Once upon a time in
Andaman

S Ashvin

INDIA • SINGAPORE • MALAYSIA

ISBN
Paperback 979-8-89699-775-7
Hardcase 979-8-89777-359-6

'Once Upon a Time in Andaman' is a science-fiction thriller narrative primarily set in the Andaman Islands, India.

Image sources:

1. https://cutt.ly/WJ7UdqX
2. https://cutt.ly/zJ7UcIv
3. https://cutt.ly/JJ7UmTF
4. https://cutt.ly/LJ7UTzg
5. https://cutt.ly/NJ7UOOx

Contents

Preface

Imagine a life where everything unfolds just as you planned, serene and steady. But then, without warning, your world turns upside down, chaos replacing calm, and you're left searching for answers. Who would you hold accountable— friends, family, or perhaps even yourself?

In the pages that follow, the journey moves across different places in Chennai and the Andaman Islands, each moment tied to its own place and time. Readers are encouraged to keep track of these shifts to stay immersed in the unfolding story. To enrich this experience, some chapters conclude with images capturing the essence of these locations, offering a glimpse into the world that shapes this tale.

"They always say time changes things, but you actually have to change them yourself."

-Andy Warhol

1. The Arrival

It was early March, the beginning of spring, around 10 in the morning. The sky was clear, and the sun shone brightly, illuminating the lush, green landscapes of the Andaman and Nicobar Islands. Birds chirped, filling the air with a lively melody, enhancing the natural beauty of these islands nestled in the Bay of Bengal, close to Myanmar. Known for their rich tourism and cultural diversity, these islands are home to a mix of communities. While most residents are Bengalis, there is also a strong presence of Tamil and Telugu-speaking people. Despite this blend of backgrounds, Hindi serves as the common language, uniting them all. Visitors come here for various reasons—whether for a joyful getaway, to explore scenic spots, for a honeymoon, or to unwind on one of Asia's cleanest beaches.

Away from the bustling city of Port Blair, a small hill rises near the seashore, its slopes largely covered in dense forest. A narrow road winds from the foot of the hill up to its summit. At the top, a small, levelled clearing hosts just two modest single-storey houses. One is a cozy 2BHK, while the other offers slightly more space as a 3BHK. The owner of the houses lived in the 3BHK, while the smaller 2BHK was available for rent. Set about a hundred meters apart, the two houses were separated by thick clusters of trees, offering a natural barrier between them. In front of each house, a concrete pathway allowed for easy vehicle access. A taxi pulled up in front of the 2BHK, and a man, dressed neatly in formal attire, stepped out, paid the driver, and moved to open the trunk to collect his luggage. Moments later, a woman wearing a striking red saree exited the taxi, pausing to adjust her hair. The pair was warmly greeted by the homeowners, Sakshi and her husband, Roy, who were standing outside, awaiting their arrival.

Sakshi is a kind-hearted and beautiful woman, known for her warmth and openness. She enjoys making new friends and treats everyone with the same respect and kindness, embodying the friendliness typical of many Andaman locals. She once worked as a bank clerk but left her job after marrying Roy. Sakshi's father served as an army officer, while her mother dedicated herself to caring for their home. Roy, her husband, is both smart and driven, working hard to expand his own business. Though their marriage was arranged, there is a deep, unspoken love between Roy and Sakshi that strengthens their bond day by day.

The man who stepped out of the taxi greeted Sakshi with a polite smile. "Good morning, I'm Vasudev, and this is my wife, Anu. We're from Chennai," he introduced, gesturing to the woman beside him. "I spoke to you on the phone yesterday about our arrival."

"Yes, I remember," Sakshi replied warmly. "It's nice to meet you both. Welcome to the Andamans! I hope you have a wonderful time here."

Vasudev is deeply passionate about science and technology. When engaged in conversation, he mostly gravitates toward scientific topics, which has led some to see him as a bit of a "crazy scientist." Often immersed in his work, he spends his free time reading books in his field of interest. His wife, Anu, manages their home and supports his unique, driven lifestyle.

"Here are the keys. Let me show you around the house," Mr. Roy said, handing them the keys and guiding Vasudev and Anu inside the 2BHK house.

The sofa, dining table, television, and other belongings had arrived just two days earlier from Chennai on a cargo ship. After a brief tour of the house, Vasudev and Anu started to get familiar with the layout. The rooms, however, were dusty and in need of a thorough cleaning, and the furniture and other items still needed to be arranged properly.

"It seems you have quite a bit of work ahead, Mrs. Anu," Sakshi remarked with a warm smile. "What are you planning to do for lunch?"

"I'll have to make it after I finish cleaning," Anu replied, her voice sounding a bit weary.

"Don't worry about it. I'll prepare lunch for both of you," Sakshi offered kindly.

At first, Anu hesitated but eventually accepted Sakshi's kind offer.

"Alright, ma'am, we'd be delighted to taste your homemade delicacies," Anu replied with a grateful smile.

"Why don't you both join us for tea in the evening once you're done with everything?" Sakshi suggested warmly.

"Sure, we'd be happy to join you after I finish tidying up," Anu replied cheerfully.

"Alright then, carry on with your work. I'll check in on you in the afternoon," Sakshi said before heading back to her house with Roy.

As they walked, Roy turned to her, "I need to head to work now. I'm already running late." He hurried to his car, parked in a nearby shed, waved goodbye to Sakshi, and drove off to his workplace.

Anu and Vasudev began organizing their belongings around the house. Anu picked up a broom and started sweeping the floors while Vasudev wandered from one room to another.

"What are you looking for, Vasu?" Anu asked, watching him curiously.

"Just a good spot to set my things up," Vasudev replied with a hint of excitement.

After settling on a spot in one of the rooms, Vasudev began moving his belongings from the hall to the designated area. Carefully, he opened each piece of luggage. In one box, he found a collection of books, which he arranged neatly on a shelf, though a few had to be stacked on a nearby table due to lack of space. Another box held glass tubes and electrodes, securely wrapped in bubble wrap. He placed these aside carefully.

In a large blue bag, he unpacked his laptop, various wires, and electronic components, setting them up on a wooden table. His 27-inch LCD display was stored in a cardboard box, protected by thermocol, which he carefully unpacked and arranged. A black bag held his clothes and personal hygiene items, while another box contained a large dish that resembled a set-top box signal receiver, though it was notably larger. He affixed the dish to the window sill outside.

Finally, he retrieved some notebooks from his bags and stored them neatly in the almirah, gradually bringing order to the space and making it feel like his own.

"Why don't you help me out if you're finished with your setup?" Anu called from one of the rooms.

"I'm not done yet. You keep going," Vasudev replied, focused on setting up his computer and other equipment.

"Yeah... yeah... it's always you and your science stuff," Anu muttered in a low, frustrated tone. "Your mother sent us here so we could have some time together, some privacy, but it seems you're just as absorbed in your work here as you were in Chennai." With a sigh, she continued with her cleaning.

As the afternoon wore on and the work was nearly finished, a knock sounded at the front door. Anu opened it to find Sakshi standing there, holding a triple-decker steel lunchbox.

"I've made chicken biryani and gravy for lunch. I hope you enjoy it," Sakshi said, handing the lunchbox to Anu.

"Thank you so much," Anu replied gratefully. She was about to close the door when Sakshi stopped her, looking as if she had something important to say.

"Oh, I almost forgot to mention—there was a house robbery in our area a few days ago. Just be cautious, and make sure to lock up whenever you leave, even if it's just for a short while," Sakshi advised.

"I usually lock up with a heavy-duty lock whenever I step out. I don't think this thief will be much of a threat to us, but thanks for the reminder," Anu reassured her.

"Alright then. And don't forget to join us for tea this evening!" Sakshi reminded her with a warm smile.

"We'll definitely be there," Anu replied, returning the smile as she gently closed the door.

Feeling her hunger grow, Anu opened the lunchbox, washed the plates and spoons, and called Vasudev over for lunch.

"Not now, Anu," Vasudev replied, still engrossed in setting up his equipment.

The house was filled with the enticing aroma of the food Sakshi had brought, the scent slowly drifting into the room where Vasudev was working. The warm, spiced fragrance of chicken biryani and gravy grew stronger, momentarily pulling Vasudev's attention away from his setup.

"Ah! What a smell. Maybe I can pause my work for a bit and fill my tummy," Vasudev thought to himself, as he hurried into the dining room, where a plate of biryani awaited him. He sat down, took a spoonful, and savored it slowly.

"Wow! This biryani is delicious. You've never made biryani like this before," Vasudev remarked, clearly impressed.

"Really?" Anu asked, a hint of tension flickering across her face.

"What's wrong? You seem a bit anxious," Vasudev observed.

"Ah… it's nothing, Vasu. Sakshi mentioned there's a thief in the area, so I'm just feeling a little uneasy," Anu replied, hesitating slightly.

"Don't worry, dear. Andaman is a small place. The thief won't be able to dodge the cops for long—they'll catch him sooner or later. For now, let's just enjoy this amazing food our neighbor prepared," Vasudev said reassuringly, smiling as he continued eating.

After finishing his meal, Vasudev returned to his work, while Anu remained at the dining table, lost in thought. Her fingers idly rested on her plate, where some biryani still remained, her mind drifting as she stared off in quiet contemplation.

Fig 1: A map of India for reference

2. Birth of An Evil

A man sprinted through the fading light, a heavy bag of cash slung over his shoulder. His eyes darted around, scanning for a safe place to hide. Suddenly, the sound of an approaching police jeep pierced the quiet evening. Panicked, he veered off the road and slipped into the dense forest, crouching low among the trees as the jeep rumbled past.

As the sun dipped below the horizon, darkness quickly enveloped the area, leaving it eerily quiet and deserted. The thief waited, biding his time. Once he was certain the coast was clear, he cautiously emerged from the forest. The narrow, muddy road ahead stretched into the night, and he began walking along it, determined to find a more secure hideout.

"Finally! A successful loot after a long time," he thought, a sly grin spreading across his face. But his satisfaction was fleeting. *"This isn't enough... I need more,"* he thought, his eyes

glinting with greed as he trudged down the narrow, muddy road, plotting his next move.

As he walked along the narrow road, his foot caught on a rock, sending him tumbling sideways. Before he could react, he fell into a deep trench beside the road, landing with a loud splash in foul, stagnant water. The putrid smell hit him immediately, making him gag. Drenched from head to toe in the filthy liquid, he pinched his nose and scrambled to climb out, desperate to escape the stench.

Once he was back on solid ground, he tried to shake off the water, muttering curses under his breath. He resumed walking but stopped abruptly after a few steps. Something tugged at him. He turned around and stared into the dark, murky trench. His mind raced as shadows from his past resurfaced, haunting him with memories he had tried so hard to bury.

Ragul was born and raised in the slums of Chennai, the only child of his parents, Raj and Reema. Both worked tirelessly as sanitary workers, scraping together a modest living. Despite their humble means, they poured all their hopes into Ragul, a bright and promising student. From a young age, he excelled not only in academics but also in athletics, earning a collection of medals and trophies during his school years.

Raj and Reema toiled day and night to fund his education, dreaming of a future where Ragul's success would lift them out of hardship and bring an end to their struggles. He was their pride, their hope, and their greatest joy.

Every evening, as Raj returned home after a long day of work, Ragul would eagerly rush to greet him. His eyes sparkled with affection, but no matter how much he longed to embrace his father, he always stopped short. A pungent, overpowering smell clung to Raj, a constant reminder of his exhausting job as a sanitary worker. Ragul's heart ached with love and pride, but the odor created an invisible barrier between them.

"Why do you always smell like this when you come home, Appa?" Ragul asked one evening, his innocent eyes filled with curiosity.

Raj sighed, a weary smile on his face. "What can I do, my son? My job requires me to work in some of the filthiest places in the city," he explained, his voice heavy with both resignation and hope. "But don't worry, this too shall pass, someday." With that, he patted Ragul gently on the head and headed to the bathroom to wash away the grime of the day.

One day, it was Ragul's birthday. That morning, Raj knelt down beside his son and promised, "I'll be home early tonight so we can celebrate together." With a hopeful smile, Raj left for work, while Ragul headed to school in his worn-out uniform, unable to afford a new outfit for his special day.

As the evening arrived, Ragul returned home, eagerly waiting for his father. But as time passed and Raj still hadn't come back, Ragul's excitement turned into frustration and worry. He broke his promise, Ragul thought, clenching his fists, anger mixing with concern.

Just then, Ragul heard hurried footsteps. His mother, Reema, burst through the door, her face streaked with tears. She was crying uncontrollably, her sobs filling the small room. Ragul's heart sank. Something was terribly wrong.

"What's the matter? What happened, Amma?" Ragul asked, his voice trembling with fear.

"*Your father… your father is in very serious condition, Ragul,*" Reema sobbed, her voice cracking under the weight of her grief.

"*What? But how?*" Ragul asked, his eyes wide with shock, his voice barely above a whisper. His mind raced, struggling to process the words. The room seemed to close in around him as fear and disbelief took hold.

"*He was tasked with cleaning a deep sewer alongside three other men,*" Reema began, her voice trembling. "*I was standing nearby with some workers, helping load the waste onto a truck. Everything seemed fine at first. They were making progress. But after a while, there was no response from your father or the others inside the sewer. We called out to them, but there was only silence. Fear gripped us. We rushed to pull them out.*"

Her tears flowed freely now. "*They were all motionless, Ragul. We rushed them to the nearest hospital. The doctors said they had inhaled a toxic gas, and their condition was critical. They warned us that survival chances were slim.*"

Reema's voice broke as she continued, "*Your father… he's in a very serious condition, Ragul. I knew you'd be home by now, so I came to take you with me to the hospital.*"

"*Why did my father even agree to do such a disgusting and dangerous job?*" Ragul asked, his voice rising in anger and frustration.

Reema fell silent, her head hanging low. After a moment, she spoke softly, her words heavy with sorrow. "*I know it's a dangerous job,*" she said, her voice barely audible. "*But he wanted to give you something special for your birthday. When they offered him double the usual pay for this task, he didn't think twice. He was willing to take the risk… for you, Ragul.*"

Reema and Ragul rushed to the hospital, their hearts pounding with fear and hope. But their world crumbled when the doctor delivered the devastating news—Raj was gone. The three other men who had entered the sewer with him were also declared dead.

Reema let out a heart-wrenching cry before collapsing to the floor, unconscious. Nurses hurried to her side, trying to revive her. Ragul stood frozen, his mind unable to process the words.

The weight of the loss hit him like a tidal wave. Memories of his father flooded his mind—his warm smile, his promises, his tireless sacrifices. Unable to hold back, Ragul broke down, tears streaming uncontrollably as he cried out for the man who had been his guiding light.

From that fateful day, Ragul made a vow—to change the lives of those who risk their safety and dignity in hazardous jobs. He resolved to become an Indian Administrative Services (IAS) officer, determined to end the suffering of workers like his father.

Fueled by purpose, Ragul burned the midnight oil, dedicating himself to his studies. His hard work paid off when he topped his board exams, earning a seat at one of the state's most prestigious arts and science colleges. There, he pursued a degree in political science while simultaneously preparing for the Indian Civil Services Examination.

The college's dedicated civil services training cell provided him with essential guidance, from rigorous preparation for the exams to mock interviews. His professors admired his sharp intellect and keen insights, and he consistently excelled in the training program. Assessors praised his confidence, articulate responses, and problem-solving skills during mock interviews.

Despite his academic and career aspirations, Ragul remained an active member of the college athletics team. He regularly represented his college in intercollegiate competitions, showcasing his talent and discipline. Balancing academics and extracurricular activities, he still managed to score top marks in his semester exams.

Ragul's dynamic personality and helpful nature made him a favorite among his peers, earning their respect and admiration. He was a symbol of perseverance and hope, inspiring others with his relentless pursuit of his dreams.

One day, at the start of his second year, the results for the second semester were announced. After class, Ragul's professor called him to the front of the room, a proud smile on his face.

"Students," the professor began, his voice filled with excitement, "let's give a big round of applause for Ragul! He has not only secured the first rank in his second semester exams but has also topped the first-year exams by achieving the first rank in both consecutive semesters. This is no small feat—let's celebrate his incredible achievement!"

The classroom erupted in applause, with his classmates cheering and congratulating him. Ragul stood there, a humble smile on his face, feeling a mix of pride and gratitude for the recognition of his hard work.

It was one of the happiest moments of Ragul's life. The sound of applause and cheers filled the room, and he felt a surge of pride and joy. As the clapping died down, the professor dismissed the class and left with a nod of approval.

As soon as the professor stepped out, Ragul's classmates gathered around him, offering hearty congratulations. Some patted him on the back, while others shook his hand, expressing their admiration for his dedication and brilliance. Ragul thanked each of them, his smile reflecting both humility and happiness. In that moment, he felt truly appreciated and motivated to continue striving for excellence.

"Congratulations!" one of his classmates said with a smile, extending a hand to shake Ragul's. But before Ragul could respond, the classmate suddenly pulled out a metal water bottle from behind and delivered a forceful blow to Ragul's head.

The sharp clang echoed through the classroom, loud enough to be heard by anyone passing by. Ragul collapsed to the ground, blood streaming from his head. His shocked friends quickly rushed to his side, lifting him and carrying him to the nursing room, where he received first aid.

Despite their best efforts, the injury was severe, and Ragul was taken to the hospital. There, doctors treated the deep gash, stitching it up with 16 stitches. Meanwhile, one of Ragul's friends, determined to hold the attacker accountable, set out to find the classmate. However, the culprit had disappeared. Knowing who was responsible, the friend reported the incident to the Head of the Department (HOD), filing a formal complaint.

The next day, swift action was taken. The classmate was summoned, and after an inquiry, was suspended from the college for his violent behavior.

Ragul was advised by the doctor to rest for a week. During this time, his mother cared for him, ensuring he recovered both physically and emotionally. Once healed, Ragul returned to college, determined not to let the incident derail his aspirations. He picked up right where he left off, continuing his studies with renewed focus and resilience.

In the final year of his course, Ragul's life took an unexpected and drastic turn. One evening, as he walked home from college, a sharp, searing pain shot through his head, unlike anything he had felt before. It was as if a crushing migraine had struck him out of nowhere. His vision blurred and slowly darkened until he collapsed onto the ground, unconscious.

When Ragul regained consciousness, he found himself in a hospital bed, surrounded by the sterile hum of medical equipment. His friends had brought him there, but he had no recollection of what happened after he passed out. He tried to speak, to ask what had happened, but when he called out his friend's name, no sound came from his mouth. His lips moved, but his voice had vanished.

Panicking, Ragul tried again, but every attempt was met with silence. His friends stood by, concerned but unaware of his struggle to communicate. The fear in his eyes caught the attention of a nearby nurse, who quickly informed the doctor. After a brief examination, the doctor recommended an MRI scan to determine the cause of his sudden collapse and loss of speech.

The MRI scan was complete. Ragul lay in a semiconscious state on a fowler bed in the casualty ward, unaware of the conversation happening just outside.

Reema, her face pale with worry, stood before the doctor. "What happened to my son?" she asked, her voice trembling, tears streaming down her cheeks.

The doctor sighed, his expression grave. "He's stable now, but..."

"But what?" Reema's voice rose in desperation, her hands trembling.

The doctor hesitated, choosing his words carefully. "The scan revealed significant damage to the frontal lobe of his brain. It appears to be the result of an old head injury, likely from the incident he had long ago. This damage has affected his ability to speak and... may also lead to changes in his behavior. I'm very sorry to say this."

Reema's heart sank. She clutched her saree tightly. "Can he be cured?" she asked, her voice barely above a whisper.

The doctor paused, his expression heavy with empathy. "I'm afraid not," he said gently. "The damage is extensive, and, unfortunately, beyond medical repair. I know this is difficult, but it's important to approach the situation with patience and sensitivity."

Reema nodded weakly, her tears flowing silently, as she tried to summon the strength to face this heartbreaking reality.

Lying on the fowler bed, Ragul overheard every word of the conversation between his mother and the doctor through the slightly open door. Tears welled up in his eyes and streamed down his cheeks. The weight of the doctor's words crushed him, and a deep sense of despair engulfed him.

Moments later, Reema entered the casualty ward, her face composed despite the turmoil inside her. "Everything will be alright, son. Don't cry," she said softly, trying to comfort him.

But Ragul's anger and frustration boiled over. He grabbed a notebook and pen from his bag, hastily scribbling down a message: I heard what the doctor said. Don't lie to me. I will never be alright! He held the notebook up for her to see.

Reema's heart broke as she read his words. Still, she tried to reassure him. "Don't believe his words. Believe in the Almighty. He will find a cure for you," she said gently, her voice trembling.

Ragul's anger intensified. His grip on the pen tightened until, with a sudden snap, he broke it in two. His tear-filled eyes burned red as he gave his mother a fierce, unyielding stare. Reema, shaken but silent, realized there was nothing more she could say in that moment.

She quietly turned and left the casualty ward, her composure crumbling as she began to sob uncontrollably just outside the door.

"Why did this happen to me? How?" Ragul's mind raced with questions, each more painful than the last. The weight of his thoughts pressed heavily on him, and he found himself spiraling deeper into despair. As the minutes passed, his overthinking triggered another sharp pain in his head. He winced, pressing his right palm against the throbbing spot, trying to ease the discomfort.

Suddenly, a flash of memory hit him—vivid and unmistakable. He remembered the head injury he had suffered two years ago, the moment that had changed everything. The incident replayed in his mind, and in that instant, the pieces fell into place. He knew who was responsible for his current state.

Ragul's sorrow quickly turned to rage. His eyes hardened with resolve as a single thought consumed him, to punish that person for his current state. Driven by the burning desire for revenge, Ragul vowed to confront the one who had stolen his voice.

After a day in the hospital, Ragul returned home with a prescription for medications to manage his recurring headaches. But life was no longer the same. The constant pain clouded his focus, making it difficult to concentrate on his studies. His performance in academics suffered, and his once-impressive grades began to slip.

The headaches also affected his athletic abilities. Once a star on the college athletics team, Ragul now struggled to keep up. His coach, seeing his decline, had no choice but to remove him from the team.

Late at night, as he lay in bed, memories of his past haunted him. He recalled the confidence with which he had once spoken during mock interviews, his sharp, articulate responses impressing even the toughest assessors. He remembered the thrill of winning competitions, the sense of pride and accomplishment that had defined his life.

But now, everything felt distant, almost like it belonged to someone else. The contrast between who he was and who he had become was unbearable. Each memory sharpened the edges of his pain, but more than anything, it fueled his anger.

His thoughts spiraled toward one goal: Vengeance. The desire for retribution consumed him, pushing aside everything else. He would not rest until the person who had ruined his life paid the price.

One morning, as Ragul was getting ready for college, he quietly tried to slip a hammer into his bag. But Reema, ever watchful, noticed.

"Why are you taking this hammer to college, Ragul?" she asked, her tone filled with suspicion.

Ragul hesitated for a moment, then decided not to lie. He grabbed a sheet of paper, scribbled down his reason, and handed it to her.

Reema's eyes widened as she read the words, her expression shifting from shock to anger. Without a word, she crumpled the paper and threw it aside. In a swift motion, she slapped Ragul across the face, her voice trembling with both fear and fury.

"Are you mad?" Reema yelled, her voice echoing through the room. "Do you really think that doing something like this will make you normal again? Nonsense! What are you planning to become, a rowdy? Have you lost your mind? Don't let such thoughts poison you!" Her words were laced with both fear and anger. "Have you forgotten your goals, your ambitions? Do you even understand the magnitude of pain I'm carrying in my heart right now? Every single day, I'm worrying, praying, hoping to find a cure for you."

She paused, her voice breaking. Reema walked toward the photo of Raj hanging on the wall. Gazing at it with tear-filled eyes, she whispered, "Ragul, I already lost your father a few years ago, and the pain of his absence never leaves me. Now, with what you're planning, you'll end up in jail. Is that what you want? Do you want me to lose you too?"

Her words struck Ragul like a thunderbolt. He lowered his head, guilt washing over him.

Reema turned back to him, her expression softening but still firm. "What has happened to you, Ragul? You weren't like this before. This anger is consuming you, changing you. I understand your pain, your frustration, but this—" she gestured toward the hammer, "—this is not the way. Violence won't solve anything. Think calmly, and you'll find a better way to deal with your anger."

She stepped closer, her voice now filled with pleading. "Focus on your goals, your studies, and the future you dreamed of.

Promise me, Ragul, that you won't let these violent thoughts take over again. Promise me you'll fight this darkness the right way."

Ragul hesitated, his mind a storm of conflicting emotions. Reema's angry yet expectant gaze didn't waver. After a moment, she softened her tone and said gently, "If you have love and respect for me, then promise me."

Ragul slowly raised his right hand and placed it on his mother's head, silently making the promise she needed to hear.

Reema nodded approvingly. "Good. Now go to college and focus only on your studies. Nothing else matters," she said firmly.

Ragul picked up his bag and walked out of the house, his steps slow and heavy. But things were not the same anymore. His mind remained clouded, and he struggled to regain his former focus. The weight of his condition and the bitterness of his shattered dreams gnawed at him. His performance in his final semesters suffered, and though he graduated, it was with great difficulty.

He let go of his dream of becoming an IAS officer. His sole aim now was to find a cure for his disability and reclaim some semblance of normalcy.

After graduation, Ragul took a job as a typist in a small job typing center, earning just enough to cover his basic needs. Days turned into months, and a year passed by, his life marked by routine and a lingering hope for healing.

One day, while at work, Ragul flipped through a local newspaper during a break. His eyes caught an advertisement for a hospital announcing the visit of renowned brain specialists from the USA that weekend. The ad highlighted their expertise in performing highly complex brain surgeries.

"Maybe I can find a cure here," Ragul thought, a flicker of hope igniting in his heart. Without wasting a moment, he emailed the hospital's contact listed in the advertisement and secured an appointment.

The following day, Ragul made his way to the hospital, located in the heart of the city—a half-hour journey from his workplace. The hospital bustled with activity, a mix of patients and medical staff moving about.

After checking in, Ragul was directed to meet Dr. Kapil, a highly experienced brain specialist with a reputation for successfully handling complicated cases over the past 25 years. Sitting across from the doctor, Ragul felt a mix of nervousness and anticipation, hoping this could be the turning point in his life.

"You must be Ragul. Tell me, what seems to be the problem?" Dr. Kapil asked, his tone calm and professional.

Ragul, prepared for this moment, handed over a piece of paper detailing his condition along with the scan reports from his previous treatment. Dr. Kapil carefully read through the note and examined the reports for a few minutes.

"Ragul," he began, looking up, "the frontal lobe of your brain has sustained significant damage due to trauma. This explains your loss of speech. Your case is complex, but there's good news— you can be cured."

Hearing this, Ragul's face lit up with a hopeful smile.

Dr. Kapil continued, smiling gently, "You'll need to undergo a surgery that involves repairing the damaged neurons in your brain. Once the procedure is successful, you should regain your ability to speak."

But then, his tone shifted. "However," he added, "the surgery is expensive. It will cost around fifty lakh rupees. I hope you have the necessary funds."

Ragul's smile vanished instantly. The weight of the amount hit him hard. Without a word, he left the hospital, disappointment etched on his face.

As he walked slowly down the bustling street, the sounds of people chatting happily across the road only deepened his sadness. Tears welled up in his eyes and streamed down his cheeks, each drop carrying the weight of his shattered hopes.

Months went by, and Ragul juggled two typing jobs to increase his income, hoping to save enough for his treatment. Life was exhausting but his determination kept him going.

One morning, on his way to work, he noticed a crowd gathered in a local park. Curious, he stepped inside to see what was happening. A charity event was in full swing. On the stage, a man was distributing clothes and money to the underprivileged. The crowd erupted in applause as people received the donations, and nearby, a few media personnel captured the event, clicking photographs and recording footage.

Ragul's eyes shifted to a large banner on the stage, which read "Charity Event by The People's Society" in bold letters. It didn't take long for him to realize that the man at the center of all the praise and generosity was none other than Mr. Gopal, the owner of Gopal Jewelries, one of the most renowned jewelry chains in the city. Mr. Gopal was the chief guest for the event, which was organized by the NGO, The People's Society.

Ragul stood there, observing the scene, a mix of admiration and contemplation crossing his face.

After distributing the clothes and money, Mr. Gopal stepped up to the podium, his voice calm yet commanding as he spoke into the microphone.

"It is an immense pleasure to meet you all here today. Thank you for inviting me to this event," he began. "Helping the needy has always been my top priority. When I was asked to be a part of this initiative, I didn't hesitate for a moment. I'm glad I could make a small difference today, and I promise to continue supporting more people in the future."

He paused briefly, letting his words sink in before continuing. "I don't expect anything in return. The only reward I seek is the smile on their faces. That smile means everything to me, and it's what drives me to keep giving back. Thank you once again for this opportunity."

The crowd erupted into applause, their admiration for Mr. Gopal palpable. His words had clearly struck a chord with everyone present.

Ragul, standing quietly at the back, couldn't help but smile. "He seems like a truly generous person," he thought. "Maybe he could help me if I explain my situation." The idea brought a glimmer of hope to his weary heart.

Determined to meet Mr. Gopal, Ragul tried his best to approach him after the charity event but was unable to get through the crowd. Undeterred, he asked around and soon discovered where Gopal lived—a grand villa near Marina Beach in Chennai. Given Gopal's prominence, finding his address wasn't difficult.

The next day, Ragul made his way to the villa, only to be stopped at the gate by the security guard. "Sir is not home," the guard informed him curtly. Disappointed but resolute, Ragul returned the following day, hoping for better luck. Again, the guard turned him away.

Despite these setbacks, Ragul refused to give up. He believed deep in his heart that Gopal would help if he could only meet him.

On the third day, Ragul showed up once more, and as before, the security guard confronted him. "Why do you keep coming back? What do you want?" the guard asked, his tone laced with irritation.

Ragul joined his hands in a pleading gesture, silently requesting to meet Mr. Gopal.

Sighing, the guard picked up his phone and called Gopal. "Sir, there's a mute guy here who insists on meeting you," he said, glancing at Ragul with annoyance.

After a brief conversation, the guard ended the call and turned to Ragul. "Sir is busy right now. He doesn't have time for you. Come back later," he said harshly. "Now, go away."

Ragul was not ready to give up. Desperation overcame him as he fell to his knees, touching the security guard's feet, silently begging for just a few moments with Gopal. But the guard sneered, pushing him away roughly. "Get lost!" he barked, grabbing a cane stick and waving it menacingly. He began driving Ragul away, swatting at him as though he were an animal.

Ragul stumbled backward, his silent cries ignored. Just as he was being forced out, he glanced up and caught sight of Mr. Gopal standing by a window, his face cold and indifferent. Their eyes met for a brief moment, but Gopal did nothing. He simply turned away, leaving Ragul to his humiliation.

In that instant, Ragul's image of Gopal shattered. The man who had appeared so kind and generous during the charity event was nothing more than a façade. Behind closed doors, he was arrogant, mean, and utterly unkind.

Ragul's blood boiled with rage. His hands clenched into fists as he wiped away his tears. He turned and walked away, pretending he hadn't seen Gopal, but his mind raced with fury.

"So, all that charity work was just a publicity stunt!" he thought bitterly. "Gopal, I know exactly how to deal with people like you. You'll regret the way you treated me today. I'll make sure of it."

His determination hardened into a steely resolve as he left, plotting his next move.

In the dead of night, at 1:00 a.m., when the world around him was steeped in silence, Ragul made his move. He crept around to the back of Gopal's villa, where the shadows hid him from sight. The security guard, fighting off sleep, sat slouched in a chair near the main gate, unaware of the intruder slipping past him.

Ragul wore rubber gloves, ensuring he left no trace of his presence. A knife was tucked into his pocket, and a bag hung over his shoulder. He located a drainage pipe, climbed it with careful precision, and reached the first floor of the villa. A small bathroom window was left slightly ajar—just enough for him to slide through and enter the house.

Once inside, he moved silently, the dim moonlight filtering through the windows guiding him. His eyes scanned every room, his ears keen for the slightest sound. He searched systematically, careful not to disturb anything that might alert the household.

Finally, in one of the rooms, he found a metal almirah. His heart raced as he approached it. Gently, he tugged at the handle, expecting resistance. To his surprise, the door swung open with ease. Inside was a treasure trove—stacks of cash and glittering jewels.

Ragul's eyes lit up with excitement. His earlier rage was momentarily replaced by exhilaration. Without hesitation, he began filling his bag, his movements deliberate and quiet. The weight of the bag grew heavier, but so did his sense of satisfaction. For Ragul, this wasn't just theft—it was retribution.

As Ragul continued filling his bag, a pair of bangles slipped from his hand, landing on the floor with a soft clink. He froze, his heart pounding in his chest.

In another room, Gopal's wife, Meera stirred. Whether it was the faint sound or sheer coincidence, she woke up. Still drowsy, she got out of bed and shuffled toward the dressing room, mumbling about checking the almirah. Gopal, heavily drunk, remained in a deep sleep, oblivious to the movement around him.

Hearing footsteps approaching, Ragul quickly closed the almirah and darted behind the door, holding his breath. The darkness of the room offered him a slim advantage.

Meera entered, her movements sluggish. She walked straight to the almirah and pulled the handle. It opened easily. She frowned slightly, but in her drowsy state, she didn't notice the missing cash and jewels. The dim light in the room masked the emptiness inside.

She simply closed the almirah, reached up to grab the key from the top, locked it, and placed the key back in its spot. Satisfied, she yawned and turned to leave, heading back to her room.

Ragul remained perfectly still, waiting until her footsteps faded and the house was silent once more. Only then did he let out a slow, shaky breath, his mind racing. He knew he couldn't risk staying any longer.

Once Meera returned to her room, Ragul wasted no time. He retrieved the key from the top of the almirah, unlocked it again, and resumed filling his bag with cash and jewels. When the bag was full, he carefully locked the almirah, placed the key back in its original spot, and made his way out of the house through the same bathroom window he had entered.

As he climbed out, his vest snagged on a nail protruding from the windowsill. He yanked it free, but the sudden force caused him to lose his balance. He tumbled down into the backyard, landing with a dull thud on the grass. Though the fall left him with a few minor bruises, he quickly got up, brushing off the dirt.

The sound of his fall stirred the drowsy watchman from his chair. The man grabbed his flashlight and began walking toward the backyard to investigate.

Ragul's heart raced as he crouched low, moving swiftly and silently. Just as the watchman neared the spot, Ragul slipped out of the backyard and disappeared into the night, leaving no trace of his daring heist.

The next morning, as Meera opened the almirah to take out some jewelry, her eyes widened in horror. The shelves that once held her prized jewels and stacks of cash were empty. She let out a piercing scream, her voice echoing through the villa.

Hearing the commotion, Gopal rushed to the room. He found Meera crying hysterically in front of the open almirah. His eyes followed hers, landing on the empty space where their valuables had been. Shock and disbelief washed over him. Without wasting a moment, Gopal pulled out his cellphone and called the police.

Within minutes, two police jeeps arrived at the villa's main gate. Inspector Naidu stepped out, a tall man with a stern expression, followed by a team of constables and a dog squad. The officers quickly fanned out, searching for clues in and around the house.

Naidu entered the room, his sharp eyes immediately noticing the almirah. He approached it, his hands on his hips, inspecting the scene closely. Gopal and Meera stood beside the almirah, their faces a mix of fear and confusion.

He turned to Gopal. "Let's start from the beginning. What exactly happened, and how did you realize you'd been robbed?"

Gopal sighed. "I was getting ready for work as usual when I suddenly heard my wife screaming from this room. I rushed here and found her crying in front of the open almirah. That's when I saw everything was gone."

Naidu nodded, then addressed both of them. "You should've locked the almirah and kept the keys somewhere safe before sleeping."

Gopal quickly passed the blame. "Actually, sir, locking the almirah is my wife's responsibility."

Meera's eyes flared. "Excuse me? Gopal, I did lock the almirah last night. I'm absolutely certain of it. How could the valuables disappear from a locked almirah?"

Gopal crossed his arms, his tone growing accusatory. "Only we know where the key is kept. So, if the valuables are missing, you must know something about it."

Meera gasped, her voice rising in disbelief. "What? Are you seriously accusing me of stealing from my own home? Don't you trust me? From the way you're speaking, it sounds like you could be the mastermind behind this theft!"

Gopal's face darkened with anger. "Why on earth would I steal from my own house, you idiot?"

"The same question goes to you, Mr. Gopal!" Meera shot back, her anger flaring.

The argument between the couple escalated, with accusations flying back and forth. Inspector Naidu stood there, silently watching, before finally letting out an exasperated sigh. He facepalmed and then raised his voice.

"Will you both stop fighting!" Naidu yelled, his tone firm and commanding. "If you were planning to solve this between yourselves, why did you even bother calling me?"

The room fell into a tense, pin-drop silence. Meera and Gopal exchanged awkward glances but said nothing.

Naidu adjusted his cap and continued. "Let me do my job. I'll find out who's responsible for this theft." With that, he turned and left the room.

At the main gate, Naidu approached the security guard. "Did you notice anyone entering or leaving the house last night?" he asked, scrutinizing the guard's expression.

The guard quickly replied, "No, Sir. I didn't see anyone. I was awake the whole night. However," he hesitated for a moment, "I did hear some noises coming from the backyard late at night. When I went to check, there was no one there."

Naidu's eyes narrowed. "No one, huh? What kind of noise?"

"Sounded like something fell, Sir," the guard replied, scratching his head. "But when I looked around, everything seemed normal, so I didn't think much of it."

Naidu nodded slowly, his mind already piecing together the details.

Inspector Naidu pieced the clues together, suspecting the thief had entered the villa from the backyard. As he pondered, a constable's voice rang out, "Sir, we found something here!"

Naidu hurried to the spot to see a bangle lying on the grass in the backyard. The police dogs sniffed it eagerly, their behavior confirming it had recently been handled. Naidu concluded that the bangle must have fallen from the thief's bag during the escape. His eyes then shifted upward, spotting an open window on the first floor.

He frowned, pointing toward the pipe running up the wall. "It looks like the thief climbed the drainage pipe and entered through that window," he muttered.

Turning to his team, he issued a command. "Constable, bring the dog squad to the first floor."

Inside, Naidu went straight to the bathroom on the first floor. The faint muddy footprints on the tiled floor caught his eye. His gaze moved to the windowsill, where a small piece of cloth was stuck on a nail.

"Interesting," Naidu murmured as he examined the evidence. The dogs were brought in and immediately picked up the thief's scent from the footprints and the piece of fabric. They began barking and acting restlessly, clearly on to something.

Naidu didn't waste a second. "Follow the dogs!" he ordered, stepping aside as the dog squad led the way, their noses tracing the scent. The officers followed closely, determined to track down the thief.

The dogs followed the scent trail, leading Naidu and his team to a nearby slum. They stopped in front of a small, humble house, barking loudly.

"I believe the thief is hiding here," Naidu said, standing at the threshold. He turned to two constables. "You both go inside and bring him out. I'll wait here."

Inside the house, Ragul heard the commotion. The sound of footsteps and barking dogs sent a chill down his spine. Realizing the police were outside, he quickly hid behind a wall, covering himself with a large basket. Meanwhile, Reema sat near the main door, peeling garlic, unaware of the approaching trouble.

Without knocking, the constables burst into the house, startling Reema. One of them addressed her curtly, "We need to search your house."

Reema looked up, confused and alarmed. "What's going on? Why are you—"

Before she could finish, the constables began rummaging through the house. They searched every corner methodically until one of them uncovered a bag hidden beneath a pile of clothes. Opening it, they found stacks of cash and glittering jewels.

"Sir, we've found the stolen items," one constable reported to Naidu over the walkie-talkie.

Reema gasped, her eyes widening in disbelief as she stared at the bag. "This… this isn't ours! I don't know how it got here!" she exclaimed, her voice trembling.

The constables ignored her protests. "You are under arrest. We need to take you in for questioning," one of them said firmly.

"Please, Sir, I swear I don't know anything about this!" Reema pleaded, her hands folded in desperation. "I didn't do anything wrong. Please don't arrest me!"

"Whatever you have to say, save it for the station," the constable replied coldly. "Now, come with us."

As the constables tried to forcibly drag Reema out, she screamed for help, her voice filled with fear and desperation. Ragul, still hidden, could hear every word. His blood boiled as he listened to his mother's cries. He couldn't stand it any longer.

Overcome with rage, Ragul leapt out from his hiding spot, grabbing a knife from a nearby shelf. Without thinking, he charged at the constable who was holding his mother, his anger blinding him to everything else.

"Ragul, no!" Reema cried, seeing her son's intentions. She tried to intervene, stepping between him and the constable, but Ragul, consumed by fury, didn't stop. As he swung the knife in the constable's direction, the officer sidestepped just in time.

In the chaos, Ragul's second attempt to strike missed the officer entirely and, instead, plunged into Reema's chest as she tried to shield the constable. The room froze. Ragul stood stunned, his hand still gripping the knife, as Reema gasped in pain, her eyes wide with shock.

"What have you done?" Reema whispered, tears streaming down her face. "Will you never listen to me?" Her voice was weak, and she stumbled, collapsing to the floor.

The constables, equally shocked, scrambled to call for backup. One officer shouted into his walkie-talkie, summoning the others waiting outside. Within moments, the house was swarming with police.

Realizing the gravity of what had just happened, Ragul panicked. Fear overtook his anger. He dropped the knife, his hands trembling, and without a second glance, fled the scene through a back window. The sound of officers shouting and Reema's labored breathing filled the air as Ragul disappeared into the maze of the slum, leaving behind his critically injured mother and the stolen bag of valuables.

Ragul darted through the labyrinth of narrow streets, his breath coming in quick, shallow bursts. The sound of heavy boots thudded behind him as the cops pursued, their shouts echoing through the cramped alleyways. With no space for vehicles, the chase continued on foot.

He leapt over walls, scaled the roofs of small houses, and twisted through back alleys, his every move driven by desperation. But the police were relentless, spreading out and blocking every obvious escape route. Ragul's pulse pounded in his ears, each beat louder than the last, his heart threatening to burst from his chest.

The sharp pain in his head struck again, slowing him slightly, but his will to escape overpowered the pain. He pressed on, pushing his body beyond its limits.

As the city noise faded behind him, Ragul found himself near the harbor. The sound of waves crashing against the dock and the distant hum of cargo ships filled the air. His eyes darted around for a hiding place.

Spotting a stack of intermodal containers, Ragul ran toward them. He climbed over one and found a small hole in the corner of a rusted container. Without hesitation, he squeezed himself inside, his body trembling as he curled up in the cramped, dark space.

The muffled sound of police sirens grew fainter, but Ragul remained motionless, his breathing ragged. The pain in his head pulsed, but for now, he was hidden. He had no idea how long he could stay there, but at least for the moment, he had evaded capture.

The cops arrived at the harbor just seconds after Ragul had disappeared into the maze of containers. They spread out, searching every nook and cranny, but Ragul was nowhere to be found. Their vision swept across the stacks of intermodal containers, but the labyrinthine layout of the harbor made the search difficult.

Meanwhile, a mobile harbor crane roared to life nearby, its massive arm reaching down to pick up one of the containers. Unbeknownst to the police, it was the very container in which Ragul was hiding. The crane operator, following routine loading procedures, lifted the container high into the air and moved it over to a cargo ship preparing for departure.

With a heavy clank, the container was secured onto the ship, which was bound for the Andaman Islands. Ragul, curled up inside, felt the sudden jolt of movement but stayed silent, realizing that he was now being taken far from the city—and the reach of the police.

The ship's engines rumbled to life as it prepared to set sail, leaving the cops behind on the dock, frustrated and unaware of Ragul's accidental escape plan.

As the vivid memories of his past faded, Ragul's mind returned to the present. His steps faltered, and his eyes filled with tears. The weight of his actions and the pain he had caused his mother pressed heavily on his heart.

"*Please forgive me, Amma,*" he whispered silently in his thoughts, his head bowed in remorse.

With each step, his guilt grew. Wiping away the tears, he continued walking slowly, unsure of where his path would lead but determined to carry the burden of his past with him.

Fig 2: Chennai harbour

3. Post-crime Investigations

Inspector Varun arrived at the crime scene in the evening, his jeep pulling up beside the single-story house near the roadway. Four constables followed him, stepping out to assess the situation. The looted house stood out among the nearby residences, its front door ajar. Varun immediately noticed the broken latch and a shattered lock lying on the ground. The thief had clearly capitalized on the house being locked and empty.

A small crowd had gathered outside, murmuring among themselves and observing the scene from a distance. Varun approached them, his tone authoritative yet calm.

"Who called the cops?" he asked.

A man stepped forward from the crowd. "I did, Sir. This is my house. My name is Ratnakar."

Varun nodded. "Tell me exactly what happened."

Ratnakar sighed heavily. "Sir, when I returned home from work, I saw that the lock on my front door was smashed. I rushed inside and found my almirah open, with clothes scattered everywhere. The locker inside was broken, and all my savings were gone. I usually keep my daily earnings in that locker."

"Where do you work?" Varun asked.

"I own a grocery store in Aberdeen Bazaar," Ratnakar replied.

"Do you have any CCTV cameras installed in or around your house?"

Ratnakar shook his head. "No, Sir. But after this incident, I think it's high time to get one."

Varun entered the house, scanning the disarray. The almirah and its broken locker were just as Ratnakar had described. He returned outside and turned to the crowd.

"Was anyone here when this happened?" he asked.

A man in the group replied, "Sir, we were all at work during the day. None of us knew about the robbery until we got back."

Varun nodded thoughtfully. "The thief likely struck around midday, knowing the area would be empty. It seems they had been watching your routine, Ratnakar. They must have known you were carrying a significant amount of money and timed the robbery accordingly."

Ratnakar's face grew tense. "Please, Sir, recover my money. It's all I have."

"How much was stolen?" Varun asked.

"About five lakh rupees," Ratnakar replied angrily. "That thief took everything!"

"Don't worry. File a First Information Report (FIR) at the station, and we'll begin the investigation," Varun assured him.

With that, Varun and his team returned to the jeep, heading back to the police station. Ratnakar followed shortly after to file the complaint.

Once at the station, Ratnakar was handed a sheet of paper to write his complaint. As he scribbled down the details, Inspector Varun's mind churned with questions. Something about the case felt personal, deliberate.

"Do you have any suspicions? Maybe a regular customer or someone you know?" Varun asked, breaking his silence.

Ratnakar let out a nervous chuckle. "No, Sir. I have many regular customers at my shop. It's impossible to suspect them all."

"Alright," Varun said, leaning back slightly. "If anything or anyone comes to mind, let us know immediately. It'll help us narrow down the suspect."

"Of course, Sir. It's my money on the line," Ratnakar replied, his tone resolute. He left the station after receiving permission, promising to stay in touch.

As the door closed behind Ratnakar, Varun ordered a constable to bring him a glass of tea. Minutes later, the tea arrived. Varun sipped it slowly, deep in thought. His eyes drifted to the stack of complaint files on his desk.

He flipped through the day's registered cases, his mind piecing together clues. Somewhere among these reports, he hoped to find the thread that would lead him to the elusive thief.

Fig 3: Aberdeen Bazaar, Port Blair

4. Tea-time Talks

Present day, at evening.

Vasudev and Anu arrived at Sakshi's house for tea, as invited. When they knocked on the door, it was opened by an elderly woman.

"A pleasant evening to both of you. Please, come in," she said warmly. It was Sakshi's mother, Geetha. She was a frail, thin woman with snow-white hair, her arms trembling slightly from age-related ailments.

Vasudev returned her smile and greeted her. "Good evening. Where is Mr. Roy?" he asked politely as they stepped inside.

Geetha gestured toward the hallway. "He's on his way home. Please, make yourselves comfortable in the hallway and wait for a little while. I've got a few things to finish up in the kitchen, but I'll be as quick as I can." She gave them an apologetic smile. "In the meantime, let me turn on the television for you both.".

Geetha returned to the kitchen after switching on the television, leaving Vasudev and Anu seated on the couch. While Anu quietly watched the program, Vasudev soon lost interest. His eyes wandered around the room, taking in the decorations and framed pictures on the wall.

One frame held a serene painting of a lakeview, its colors soft and calming. Next to it was a family photo, capturing Sakshi, Roy, and Geetha together, smiling warmly. Another frame displayed a portrait of Roy, his confident gaze fixed forward.

There was also a picture of Goddess Saraswathi, her divine presence radiating wisdom and grace. Finally, Vasudev's eyes rested on a portrait of a man, adorned with a garland draped around the frame. It was clear this was someone who had passed away.

That must be Sakshi's father, Vasudev thought, observing the respectful placement of the photograph. The room's quiet ambiance seemed to reflect both love and loss, creating a subtle but profound sense of family history.

A few minutes later, Roy's car pulled into the driveway. He stepped out, looking visibly tired, and hurried into the house.

"Hello, good evening," Roy greeted Vasudev and Anu briefly, managing a quick smile before heading straight to the bedroom to freshen up. After a quick shower, he changed into a comfortable t-shirt and track pants, feeling more relaxed as he returned to the hall.

By then, the tea and samosas were ready. Sakshi entered the room carrying a serving plate with a tea kettle and five cups, her smile warm and inviting. Geetha followed, carefully balancing a tray of samosas, her hands steady despite her earlier tremors.

"Tea and snacks are served!" Sakshi announced cheerfully, setting the table as everyone began to settle in for an enjoyable evening.

The five of them—Vasudev, Anu, Sakshi, Roy, and Geetha—gathered around the tea table, creating a cozy and welcoming atmosphere. Sakshi poured tea into each cup while Geetha passed around the samosas and other snacks.

"Thank you for inviting us, Aunty," Anu said with a polite smile, looking toward Geetha.

"Don't mention it, dear," Geetha replied warmly. "It's our little tradition to invite new neighbors over for tea. It's a wonderful way to get to know each other."

Roy, now more relaxed after freshening up, leaned forward slightly. "We only had a brief chat this morning," he said, addressing Vasudev. "Why don't you tell us a bit more about yourself?"

Vasudev smiled, taking a sip of tea before responding. "I was born and raised in Chennai. I'm a theoretical physicist by profession. Until recently, I was teaching at a university, but I've decided to take a break for now."

Roy's eyes lit up with interest. "A physicist? That's impressive! Nowadays, most people only think about becoming doctors, engineers, business owners, or some other high-paying professional. What inspired you to choose physics as a career?"

Vasudev took a bite of the samosa and continued, "Actually, my fascination with physics started when I was a kid. In eleventh grade, I even ranked second in a physics Olympiad exam."

Roy chuckled. "That's impressive. It's rare to meet someone who's so passionate about physics these days."

Vasudev smiled. "Thank you. So, how about your parents? Where do they live?" he asked, shifting the conversation.

"They live on Havelock Island," Roy replied. "I'm staying here in Port Blair because of work. I've asked them to move in with me several times, but they prefer staying in their hometown. It's more comfortable for them, and they've built a life there."

"How are they able to manage things there?" Vasudev asked, curious.

"My father receives a decent pension, which covers their daily expenses," Roy explained. "I also deposit a portion of my salary into their bank account regularly. Havelock Island is about an hour away by boat, so I can't visit them as often as I'd like. But whenever I get a break from my hectic schedule, I make sure to spend some time with them."

Vasudev nodded, appreciating Roy's dedication. "Where do you work, sir?" he asked.

"I run a tours and travels company," Roy replied with a hint of pride.

"Oh, that's great!" Vasudev said, smiling warmly. "You must get to meet a lot of interesting people."

"After finishing my BBA degree, I wanted to start a profitable business," Roy began, a proud smile on his face.

"Being born and raised in the Andaman Islands, I was used to seeing a lot of tourists here. That's when I thought—why not start a tours and travels company? It seemed like a fantastic idea."

He paused, taking a sip of tea. "Fortunately, the business grew significantly within five years. I started with just one Omni car, but now I own several vehicles and even a minibus. And recently, I expanded further—I now own a hotel as well," he added, his pride unmistakable.

"That's impressive," Vasudev said, genuinely admiring Roy's entrepreneurial journey. "It sounds like all your hard work really paid off."

"You seem to have built a solid business and probably have a large bank account," Vasudev said, taking another sip of tea. "Yet you live in a modest home and dress so simply."

Roy smiled humbly. "I prefer a simple way of living, Vasudev. God has blessed me with everything I need to live comfortably, and for that, I'm truly grateful. Beyond that, I believe in giving back. A portion of my earnings goes toward supporting the local community here on the islands—helping with education, healthcare, and other necessities for the native people."

"That's truly admirable, sir," Vasudev said, smiling. "I respect people who not only achieve success but also share their blessings with others."

"Please tell me more about your job," Roy said, leaning forward with interest.

"I used to be a professor at IIT Madras," Vasudev said, taking another sip of tea. "While I was teaching, I was also working on a personal project. After three years, I decided to resign so I could dedicate myself fully to it."

"Oh! So, are you currently working on your project?" Roy asked, intrigued.

"Yes, of course," Vasudev replied with a nod.

Roy leaned forward slightly. "Do you plan to continue working on it while staying here in Andaman?"

Vasudev smiled. "Actually, after our marriage, my parents thought it would be good for Anu and me to have some privacy and focus on strengthening our relationship. They suggested we live separately for a while. We also wanted to take a trip somewhere nice for our honeymoon. After considering several destinations, I felt Andaman was the perfect choice. It's beautiful, peaceful, and not too far from Chennai. Plus, it gives me a serene environment to work on my project while we enjoy our time here."

"Sir, I think his only real interest is his project—forget about the honeymoon," Anu interjected, her tone playfully sarcastic.

Vasudev chuckled. "No, no, it's not like that," he said with a laugh. "But, as always, work comes first."

"In that case," Anu replied, rolling her eyes, "maybe we should just cancel the honeymoon altogether."

Roy, Sakshi, and Geetha burst into laughter at Anu's remark.

Geetha smiled and leaned forward, offering some gentle advice. "See, Vasu, you're a family man now. It's important to spend quality time with your wife, too."

Vasudev grinned sheepishly, acknowledging the point as Anu gave him a mock stern look. The room filled with lighthearted warmth as the conversation continued.

"Yes, I understand. I'll try to improve my work-life balance," Vasudev said with a smile.

Roy nodded, then leaned in with curiosity. "By the way, you haven't told me much about the project you're working on."

Vasudev hesitated, glancing at Anu for a moment. "Actually…"

"You can tell me," Roy said with a reassuring smile. "We're friends now, right?"

Vasudev sighed softly and then spoke in a low voice. "Actually... I'm building a time machine."

Roy's eyes widened in disbelief before he let out a laugh. "What? A time machine? Seriously?" he said, chuckling.

"That's why I was hesitant to tell you," Vasudev said, his tone a bit timid.

Roy quickly composed himself, raising a hand apologetically. "Okay, okay, I'm sorry. I didn't mean to laugh. But you know, a time machine is something straight out of science fiction."

"However, science is true," Vasudev said, his tone more confident now. "There were once legends and stories about traveling to the moon or Mars—things people believed were impossible. But look at us now. There are human footprints on the moon, and serious plans to build settlements on Mars.

Tell me, wasn't the moon landing something that existed only in dreams before it became a reality?"

Roy paused, considering Vasudev's point. "Well…" he started but didn't finish.

Vasudev leaned forward slightly. "There have been numerous scientific writings on time travel. Many brilliant minds have theorized about its possibility. I've read those works extensively, and I firmly believe that time travel can be achieved."

"Oh, I see," Roy said, nodding while suppressing a chuckle, still finding the idea far-fetched.

"In the past, scientists could only hypothesize about building a time machine. But now," Vasudev said, his voice steady with conviction, "I aim to turn those hypotheses into reality."

"How exactly are you constructing your… so-called time machine?" Roy asked, raising an eyebrow.

Vasudev set his empty teacup down and leaned back slightly. "Have you heard of Ernetti?" he asked, his tone suddenly more serious.

"Who's that?" Roy asked, intrigued.

Vasudev's eyes lit up as he explained. "Ernetti was a scientist who, in the 1960s, claimed to have built a device called the 'Chronovisor.' This machine supposedly allowed him to observe events from the past, almost like watching a recording of history."

Roy leaned forward, his curiosity piqued. "You're telling me someone actually built a machine like that?"

"Yes," Vasudev replied, nodding. "Ernetti even claimed to have used the Chronovisor to witness significant events, including the extinction of the dinosaurs. Although many dismissed his work as a hoax, the concept behind his machine intrigued me and inspired me to build one. It's not time travel in the conventional sense, but it opens a doorway to observing the past."

Roy's skeptical expression softened slightly as he absorbed the information. "Interesting," he muttered, though a hint of disbelief lingered in his tone.

Anu, Sakshi, and Geetha paused their conversation and turned their attention to Vasudev, intrigued by the topic.

"In one of the books I read," Vasudev continued, "it was described that Ernetti's Chronovisor was a large machine. It had massive levers, numerous switches, and a large glass screen, which he called a viewer. The key component was a huge cathode tube that captured electromagnetic waves emitted by past events. These waves were then converted into electrical signals and displayed on the screen, allowing the user to observe historical moments."

Roy frowned slightly, leaning forward. "What exactly is a cathode tube? And electromagnetic radiation? None of this makes sense to me," he admitted with a sheepish laugh.

Vasudev smiled, appreciating Roy's honesty. "A cathode tube is a device that was commonly used in older televisions and monitors. It works by directing beams of electrons onto a screen to create images. As for electromagnetic radiation, think of it as energy waves that travel through space. They come in various forms, like radio waves, X-rays, and even visible light.

Ernetti's theory was that events from the past leave behind electromagnetic traces, and his machine was designed to detect and interpret them."

Roy nodded slowly, his brow furrowed in thought. "So, if I understand correctly, you're saying that everything that's ever happened leaves some kind of invisible trace behind? And this machine of yours can pick up on those traces?"

"Exactly," Vasudev replied, pleased with Roy's grasp of the concept.

Roy leaned back in his chair, a mix of skepticism and curiosity on his face. "I have to admit, it sounds far-fetched. But then again, so did the idea of humans flying to the moon once. If you're serious about this, I'd really like to see how it works."

"You will," Vasudev said with a confident smile. "Once it's ready."

Roy started to have doubts. "But, is it possible to view the future with this machine?" he asked, his tone both curious and skeptical.

"No, that's not possible," Vasudev replied firmly.

"But why?" Roy pressed.

Vasudev leaned forward slightly. "Because our present determines our future. Every decision we make today has a ripple effect on what happens tomorrow. The future isn't fixed—it's shaped by countless variables. We can make predictions based on patterns and probabilities, but we can't observe something that hasn't happened yet."

Roy nodded thoughtfully, still processing the explanation.

Time passed, and before they knew it, the clock struck eight.

"I believe we've been chatting for quite a while," Vasudev remarked with a laugh. "I should head back now. I've got work to finish."

Roy chuckled. "Time really does fly when you're having a good conversation. Why don't you both stay and join us for dinner?"

"Another time, perhaps," Vasudev said with a smile. "My wife's already prepared dinner for us."

"Fair enough, my friend," Roy replied, smiling warmly.

Before leaving, Vasudev turned to Sakshi. "By the way, the biryani you sent us this afternoon was fantastic."

"Oh! Thank you so much. If you loved it, I'll deliver it to you every day," Sakshi said with a playful smile. Vasudev blushed slightly at her enthusiasm.

"And, Vasudev," Roy added, "don't forget to show me your project when it's finished. I'm genuinely curious to see it."

"Of course, I will!" Vasudev said confidently.

Anu glanced at the time and nudged Vasudev gently. "Okay, Vasu, we should get going now."

Vasudev and Anu stood up, bidding Sakshi and Roy good night before heading home. As they walked, Vasudev felt a sense of happiness. He had made a new friend, and it seemed like Roy truly enjoyed their conversation and was genuinely interested in his project.

After they left, Roy chuckled, turning to Sakshi. "He's a bit of a crazy man, don't you think?"

Sakshi laughed. "Maybe, but sometimes it's the crazy ones who end up doing extraordinary things."

Later that night.

After dinner, Vasudev settled into his workspace, determined to make up for lost time. Though he had enjoyed meeting Roy and his family, a nagging thought lingered in his mind: I could have used that time to work on my project.

His desk was cluttered with notes, blueprints, and electronic components, all essential parts of his ambitious endeavor. Despite the fatigue creeping in, his motivation burned brighter. The weight of his goal—the completion of his time machine—was enough to push him past his exhaustion.

With unwavering focus, he burned the midnight oil, determined to turn his vision into reality.

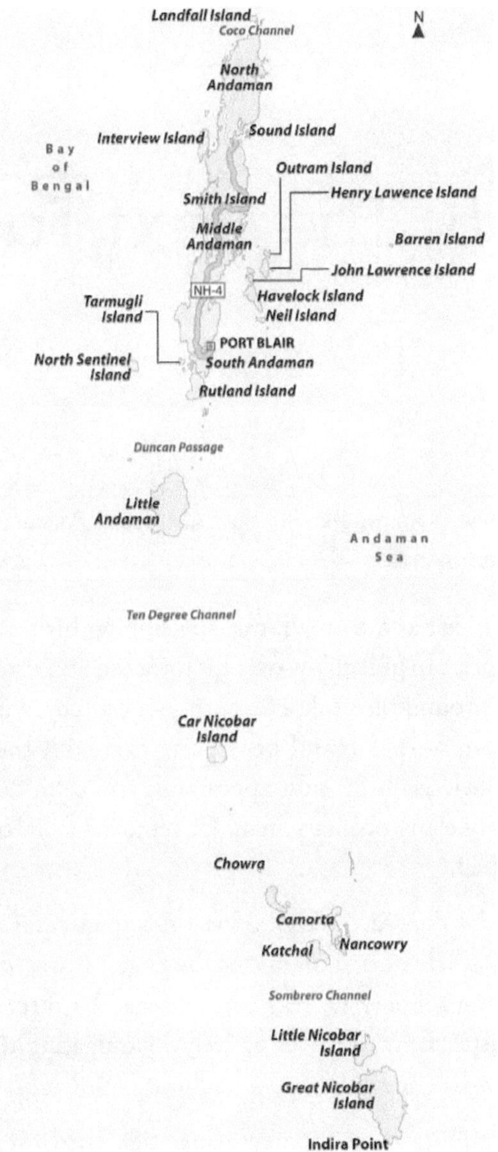

Fig 4: A map of Andaman and Nicobar Islands for reference

5. The Next Target

Next day, somewhere in the Aberdeen Bazaar, Port Blair, Andaman Islands.

Ragul sat at a tea stall, casually sipping his tea. He wore a black cap pulled low over his forehead and a scarf wrapped loosely around his neck. His outfit—a crisp brown t-shirt and black pants—was brand new, purchased with the money he had stolen. With his neat appearance and calm demeanor, he looked like any ordinary man, far removed from the image of a criminal.

As he flipped through a local newspaper, his eyes caught a small article buried on one of the pages. It was a brief report about the robbery he had committed. The piece mentioned that Inspector Varun was actively investigating the case and searching for the culprit.

Ragul's grip on the newspaper tightened for a moment, but he quickly composed himself. Finishing the last sip of his tea, he casually folded the paper, paid for his drink, and left the stall, his mind already working on his next move.

"If I stay on these islands for much longer, it's only a matter of time before I'm caught. The money I stole isn't nearly enough to achieve what I want. I need to act fast," Ragul thought, his mind racing as he wandered through the bustling streets of the Bazaar.

After hours of aimless roaming, his stomach growled, reminding him he hadn't eaten. He stopped in front of a luxurious-looking hotel called *The R's*. The two-story building exuded elegance, with large glass windows and sleek fiber-glass accents giving it a modern, upscale vibe. Ragul had never eaten at a hotel before, let alone one that looked this grand. But today, he had the means, thanks to his ill-gotten gains.

With a mix of excitement and nervousness, he walked in. A polite waiter greeted him and guided him to a table by the window. Ragul sat down, glancing around at the opulent interior before turning his attention to the menu.

His eyes scanned the options until they landed on masala dosa, a dish he had always enjoyed. But his excitement quickly faded when he saw the price—Rs. 200 for a single dosa. His brows furrowed in disbelief. *"Two hundred for a dosa?"* he thought. *"This place really knows how to empty wallets."*

Nevertheless, he decided to treat himself, reasoning that it might be the only chance he'd get to experience such luxury. He raised his hand to call the waiter, ready to indulge in his long-time wish of dining like the wealthy.

Ragul scanned the menu and pointed to the *masala dosa* with his right index finger. The waiter nodded, jotting down the order before heading to the kitchen.

As Ragul waited, he observed the bustling activity around him. The hotel was lively, filled with patrons, most of whom appeared to be tourists. While some were Indians, the majority were foreigners, chatting in various languages and enjoying their meals.

"This place is clearly a hotspot," Ragul thought. *"The owner must be making a fortune."*

The thought sparked an idea in his mind.

After finishing his meal, Ragul approached the cashier to pay. On the cash register table, he noticed a neat stack of visiting cards. Casually, he picked one up and examined it. The card displayed the name, photo, and contact details of the hotel's owner: *Roy*.

Roy, Ragul repeated in his mind, feeling a surge of excitement. The card felt like a map leading to a hidden treasure. With this new lead, he walked out of the hotel, his mind racing with plans.

As he made his way back to his hideout, Ragul began piecing together a scheme for what he believed would be his most significant and final heist.

6. The Double Lunch

It was a quiet Sunday morning. Vasudev, as usual, was immersed in his project, while Anu busied herself cleaning the house. After finishing her chores, she decided to head to the market to buy some meat. She planned to prepare biryani for lunch, knowing it would make Vasudev happy.

Meanwhile, Vasudev was making significant progress on his project. The core component—the viewer, which could display past events—was almost complete. However, he was also developing an innovative addition: a wearable device that could synchronize remotely with the time machine.

The device, resembling a sleek watch, was designed to do more than just track time. Once connected to the time machine, it would allow the wearer to actively participate in the events displayed on the viewer, effectively experiencing the past firsthand. To ensure safety, Vasudev had incorporated a failsafe—a button on the device's face that, when pressed, would immediately return the user to the present.

A few minutes after returning from the market, Anu busied herself in the kitchen, preparing lunch.

"What are you cooking, Anu?" Vasudev called out from his room, his voice echoing down the hallway.

"It's a surprise!" Anu replied with a playful tone, focusing on her task.

Three hours later, she stood at the kitchen doorway, calling out, "Lunch is ready!"

Vasudev entered the dining room a few minutes later, drawn by the delicious aroma wafting through the house. Anu began serving the food, her face glowing with anticipation.

"It smells amazing," Vasudev said, inhaling deeply.

Anu smiled, delighted by the compliment. "For lunch, I've made biryani and chicken gravy. I'm sure you'll enjoy it."

She served generous portions for both of them, and they began eating.

Anu watched anxiously as Vasudev took his first few bites. "How is it?" she asked eagerly.

Vasudev paused mid-chew, thinking for a moment. "It's not bad," he said, then added with a teasing grin, "but it's not quite like Sakshi's biryani."

Anu's face fell slightly, but before she could respond, there was a knock at the door. She stood up to answer it, brushing her hands on her apron.

Opening the door, she found Sakshi standing there, holding a tiffin box.

"Today, I made biryani for lunch," Sakshi said with a cheerful smile. "Since I know Vasudev sir enjoys it, I thought I'd bring some over for you both."

Anu hesitated, trying to hide her annoyance. "Actually, I've already prepared lunch and…"

Before she could finish, Vasudev hurried to the door, his face lighting up. He quickly took the tiffin box from Sakshi's hands. "Thank you so much, madam, for your special biryani," he said enthusiastically, completely ignoring Anu's unfinished sentence.

Sakshi smiled awkwardly, sensing the tension. "I'm sorry for disturbing you two during lunch. I'll leave now," she said, turning to walk away, clearly uncomfortable.

Vasudev barely noticed as he returned to the dining table, clutching the tiffin box like a prized possession. He opened it, scooped out some biryani, and placed it on his plate, eagerly taking a bite.

"Anu, come here and have some biryani prepared by Sakshi madam," Vasudev said, gesturing toward the tiffin box.

Anu crossed her arms, her tone sharp. "You enjoy her biryani, right? You can have the whole thing yourself."

Vasudev paused, realizing she was upset. "Oh, Anu, don't be like that. She brought it for us out of kindness. It would be rude not to accept her gesture."

Anu's eyes narrowed. "Didn't you hear what she said? She brought it because *you* like her biryani, not because we needed it." Her voice carried a mix of frustration and hurt.

"All she wants is a good relationship with us, Anu," Vasudev said, trying to sound reassuring. "Don't take it the wrong way."

But Anu remained unconvinced, her eyes subtly drifting to Vasudev's plate. She couldn't help but notice that the amount of Sakshi's biryani he had eaten was nearly double that of her own. Her heart sank a little.

"What is it, Vasudev?" she asked quietly, her voice tinged with regret. "Did you not like my biryani?"

Vasudev looked up, surprised. "I like it, Anu. In fact, I'm planning to have more for dinner. But Sakshi madam's biryani might not stay fresh until then, so I thought I'd finish hers now."

Anu sighed, trying to mask her disappointment. "Okay. As you wish," she said, resuming her meal, though her appetite seemed slightly diminished.

The rest of the meal passed in silence, the earlier light-hearted atmosphere now replaced with quiet contemplation.

Later that night.

Anu yawned, her eyelids growing heavy. Meanwhile, Vasudev remained engrossed in his project, his fingers moving deftly over his tools and notes.

Before heading to bed, Anu approached him. "When are we going back to Chennai, Vasudev? I don't think we came here just to have fun," she said, her tone tinged with impatience.

Vasudev looked up, trying to maintain a reassuring demeanor. "Anu, we've only been here a few days. Don't worry," he said with a smile. "We'll definitely go sightseeing and enjoy ourselves. There's still plenty of time. Besides, I'm so close to finishing my project. Once it's done, we can explore the islands without any stress."

Anu didn't respond. She simply nodded and walked away, heading to bed in silence.

As Vasudev watched her leave, the smile faded from his face. He could tell she wasn't convinced.

His eyes lowered to his desk, and he muttered softly, "I'm sorry, Anu. You don't know how important this project is to me."

After a brief pause, he shook his head, pushed aside his feelings of guilt, and returned to his work, the quiet hum of his tools filling the night.

7. The Big Day

Few days later, at midnight, somewhere in the islands.

Ragul lay in his safe house, exhausted after a long day of shadowing Roy, carefully noting his every move. His mind raced with thoughts of his next heist—stealing Roy's wealth and escaping the island for good. Finally, fatigue overtook him, and he drifted into a restless sleep.

Suddenly, a sharp, eerie voice pierced through the silence.

"Ragul… Ragul… How can you sleep peacefully after killing me?"

Ragul jolted awake, his heart pounding. The room was pitch black, and he couldn't see a thing. The voice was familiar, yet unrecognizable in its haunting tone.

He stood up, straining his ears, trying to pinpoint the source of the sound.

"Why are you searching for me?" the voice taunted from somewhere in the darkness.

Despite the fear crawling up his spine, Ragul moved forward, his hands outstretched, feeling his way through the dark. The voice seemed to echo from all directions, making it impossible to locate. Yet, he didn't stop. Driven by equal parts fear and determination, he continued his search, desperate to confront whoever—or whatever—was behind the voice.

"You've changed a lot," a voice echoed from the darkness, stopping Ragul in his tracks. The voice was eerily familiar, yet he couldn't place it.

He kept moving, his breaths shallow, his hands brushing against unseen obstacles in the pitch black.

"How are you going to find us if you're on the wrong path?" another voice called out, filled with disappointment.

Ragul froze. His eyes darted around, but the oppressive darkness offered no clues. Suddenly, from a distance, two figures emerged. Their faces remained hidden in shadow, but their bodies were faintly illuminated, glowing softly in the dark void.

"We believed in you," one of the figures said, their voice heavy with sorrow. "We thought you'd become someone great. But now, all that hope is gone. You've let us down."

Ragul's chest tightened as he watched. Suddenly, a faint light illuminated the faces of the two figures. His heart sank.

It was his parents—Raj and Reema. Their expressions were solemn, their eyes filled with anguish. Around their necks were nooses, swaying gently as if in a silent accusation.

"Amma... Appa..." Ragul whispered in his thoughts, unable to believe what he was seeing. His legs felt weak, and

a cold sweat dripped down his spine as the weight of his guilt pressed down on him. Without thinking, he broke into a run, desperate to reach them.

"Stop right there!" his mother's voice echoed sharply.

He froze in place, his feet rooted to the ground. Tears streamed down his face as he gazed at them, his heart heavy with guilt and sorrow.

"You are a disgrace!" his father's voice thundered, filled with anger and disappointment.

Suddenly, the solid ground beneath him disappeared. Ragul's eyes widened in terror as he plummeted into an abyss of eternal darkness. Above him, he could still see his parents, lifeless, their bodies suspended by the nooses around their necks. Their haunting eyes seemed to follow him as he fell further and further into the void.

With a gasp, Ragul jolted awake, his body drenched in sweat. He sat up abruptly, his chest heaving. He was back in his hiding place. The ground beneath him was solid, but his heart was racing, and a throbbing headache pulsed through his temples.

He clutched his head, trying to ease the pain. "*It was just a terrifying dream*," he muttered to himself in his mind, though the vivid images lingered, refusing to fade. The weight of his subconscious guilt bore down heavily, and tears began streaming down his cheeks.

After a while, Ragul wiped his face, forcing himself to focus. He couldn't afford to lose control. He needed to plan for the next day. Pushing the nightmare aside, he took an aspirin to dull the headache and lay back down, eventually drifting into a restless sleep.

Next day,

Vasudev's time machine was finally complete. The centerpiece of his invention was a dish-like receiver, designed to collect ancient electromagnetic rays lingering from past events. A diode within the machine converted these rays into electrical signals, which were then processed through two refining units to ensure clarity.

The machine featured a control knob to adjust the age of the electromagnetic waves being collected, allowing Vasudev to focus on specific periods in history. The processed signals were then displayed on a large monitor, providing a clear visual of the chosen past event. A single red button sat prominently on the console, ready to activate the viewing process.

Excitement coursed through Vasudev. This was the moment he had been working toward for years. He had promised Roy that he would demonstrate the machine once it was ready, and he was eager to fulfill that promise.

Without wasting a second, Vasudev rushed to Roy's house, his heart pounding with anticipation.

Roy was in a rush that morning, juggling his tie and briefcase as he hurried to his car. He had an important meeting with his employees and was already running behind schedule. Just as he was about to get into his vehicle, Vasudev appeared out of nowhere, his face brimming with excitement.

"Mr. Roy, please come to my house. My time machine is ready!" Vasudev exclaimed, practically bouncing on his feet.

"Not now, Vasudev," Roy replied impatiently. "I have urgent work. I really need to go."

But Vasudev wasn't about to let the opportunity slip by. Ignoring Roy's protests, he grabbed his arm. "It won't take long. You promised, remember?" Before Roy could object further, Vasudev started pulling him toward his house.

Sakshi, noticing the commotion, followed them, curious. Roy sighed heavily, his frustration growing as he checked his watch. He knew he was running late but couldn't seem to get Vasudev to listen.

As soon as they reached Vasudev's house, he wasted no time. He rushed to his workstation, turned on his computer, and began configuring the machine's settings. The hum of the machine filled the room, and a soft glow emanated from the monitor.

"Wait, this is your time machine?" Sakshi said, her eyes lighting up. "It looks amazing!"

Roy, however, was not as impressed. "I'm getting late, Vasudev. Can't we do this later?" he said, his tone laced with frustration.

"Just a few more minutes," Vasudev replied, his fingers flying across the keyboard, his excitement overriding Roy's growing impatience.

After a few final adjustments, Vasudev's time machine was ready to operate. He turned to Roy, brimming with excitement. "What would you like to see from the past?" he asked.

Roy, still glancing at his watch, replied impatiently, "Anything you want to show me, but make it quick."

"Alright then," Vasudev said, his excitement undeterred. "Let me take you back to see how Earth looked 4 million years ago."

Since it was a test run, Vasudev decided not to use the wearable device. He adjusted the knob to set the electromagnetic wave range to 4 million years and pressed the red button on the machine.

For a moment, the room fell silent. Nothing happened. Vasudev frowned and pressed the button again, this time with more force. Suddenly, the machine whirred to life, emitting a loud, persistent hum. The receiver began collecting ancient electromagnetic rays, and the viewer displayed a tab showing the proportion of rays being processed. The percentage counter slowly ticked up from zero.

Vasudev's face lit up with excitement as he watched his machine in action. "It's working!" he exclaimed.

"Congratulations, Vasudev. Your project is a success!" Sakshi said, clapping her hands lightly.

"Thank you, Sakshi madam," Vasudev replied, his smile wide with pride.

Roy and Anu stood in stunned silence, their eyes fixed on the glowing monitor, unable to look away. The hum of the machine and the rising percentage on the screen seemed to hold them spellbound.

"Surprised?" Vasudev asked Roy, a proud smile on his face.

Roy nodded, though his excitement was quickly replaced by unease as the machine continued to hum loudly.

When the processing percentage reached 5%, the machine suddenly began to vibrate violently. The lights in the room flickered erratically.

"Is everything all right?" Roy asked, his voice laced with anxiety.

Before Vasudev could respond, the ground began to shake. Roy lost his balance and fell to the floor. On the computer screen, a bright red warning tab flashed: Overload Detected.

Suddenly, the room's tube light burst with a loud crack, plunging them into partial darkness. The machine let out a groan and came to an abrupt halt. Smoke billowed from one of the processors, filling the room with the acrid smell of burning circuitry.

Sakshi and Anu gasped, stepping back in shock.

Roy scrambled to his feet, brushing himself off. His calm demeanor barely masked his irritation. "Thank you for wasting my time, Mr. Vasudev," he said coldly before storming out of the house, Sakshi following close behind.

Anu turned to Vasudev, her frustration boiling over. "Was it really necessary to show them your ridiculous project?" she snapped.

Vasudev stood there, stunned, his pride now replaced by a sinking feeling of failure. He opened his mouth to respond but couldn't find the words. His silence filled the room, heavy and suffocating.

"I warned you he was insane," Roy muttered angrily to Sakshi as they walked away, his frustration evident. He then got into his car and drove off to work.

Vasudev, standing near the window, overheard the remark. His heart sank. Embarrassment and disappointment weighed heavily on him. Years of painstaking effort now seemed wasted, crumbling in a matter of minutes.

A few moments later, Sakshi returned to the house. Seeing Vasudev's dejected expression, she walked up to him and gently placed a hand on his shoulder. "Don't worry," she said softly. "Everything will be all right. Don't take my husband's words seriously. He's in a bad mood, that's all. I believe in your machine—it'll work soon. You just need to make a few adjustments."

Her words were kind, but they barely lifted Vasudev's spirits. He managed a weak nod, appreciating her attempt to console him.

"Okay, I have to leave now," Sakshi said, glancing at the time. "I need to help my mother with some chores."

She offered a final reassuring smile to both Anu and Vasudev before leaving the house.

As the door closed behind her, Vasudev sat down, his mind clouded with doubt and frustration. The weight of failure bore down on him, making it hard to focus. *How could this happen?* he thought, staring blankly at the damaged machine. His dream, which once seemed so close, now felt farther away than ever.

"Anu, I'm not feeling well right now," Vasudev said, his voice low and somber. "I need some time alone."

Anu watched him with concern, but before she could respond, Vasudev quietly left the house, closing the door softly behind him.

Fig 5: Marina Park, Port Blair

8. An Unexpected Happening

Vasudev walked aimlessly, the weight of his thoughts heavier with each step. After covering about three kilometers, he reached Marina Park. The tranquil setting offered a temporary escape from his inner turmoil. He found an empty bench overlooking the calm waters and sat down, his head in his hands.

The day's failure played on a loop in his mind. Should I keep working on this machine, or is it just a foolish dream? he wondered, the doubt gnawing at him. For a moment, the idea of abandoning the project seemed like the easiest path. The ridicule, the setbacks—it felt like too much to bear.

But then, another thought surfaced, piercing through the fog of despair. His prime motive.

Vasudev leaned back, staring at the horizon as memories of his past flooded in. He reminded himself why he had started this journey in the first place. The stakes were too high, the purpose too significant. Giving up now wasn't an option.

As a child, Vasudev lived in Chennai with his family. His father, Selvam, owned a modest grocery shop, while his mother, Nirmala, was a dedicated homemaker. Vasudev also had a younger sister, Swathi, who was his closest companion and confidant. Whenever Vasudev felt low or isolated, Swathi was always there to lift his spirits.

Vasudev didn't have many friends growing up. His deep interest in science and constant chatter about theories and experiments made him the subject of ridicule among his peers. People often dismissed him as a nerd, and his unusual ideas only added to his isolation. The only person who listened to him without judgment was Swathi. Even though she rarely understood the complexities of what he was talking about, she would sit patiently, nodding along and pretending to grasp every word. Her unwavering support made her the one person Vasudev could always rely on.

Meanwhile, Selvam had ambitious plans to expand his grocery business. He dreamed of opening a large shopping mall in the heart of Chennai. However, the scale of the project required a significant investment, and Selvam didn't have the funds to make it happen.

In his determination to see his dream through, Selvam approached his friend Gopal, who owned a well-established jewelry store in the city. Initially, Gopal was hesitant to lend such a large sum—Rs. 10 crores. He knew the risks involved and made his concerns clear. But their friendship and Selvam's confidence eventually swayed him. Trusting Selvam's vision, Gopal handed over a cheque for the amount, cautioning him, "This is a big risk, Selvam. Make sure you don't regret it."

Selvam, brimming with optimism, assured Gopal, "Don't worry, my friend. I'll repay every penny as soon as the mall is up and running."

With the money in hand, Selvam felt unstoppable, unaware of the storm that lay ahead.

Selvam, eager to find the perfect spot for his shopping mall, approached Raghav, a well-known land broker in the city. He outlined his requirements: a large plot of land within the city limits, ideally in a bustling, populated area. After a few days of searching, Raghav returned with promising news. He had identified a piece of land that ticked all the boxes.

Selvam visited the location and immediately liked it. The area was prime, and he could envision his mall thriving there. Without hesitation, he completed the formalities and paid a hefty sum of Rs. 5 crores for the land.

A few weeks later, Selvam, his family, and a priest gathered on the land to perform rituals for the foundation stone-laying ceremony. It was a moment of pride and excitement for Selvam, a symbolic step toward realizing his dream.

However, the ceremony was interrupted when a convoy of cars arrived unexpectedly. From one of the cars emerged a man named Raja, flanked by his associates. With an air of authority, Raja strode toward Selvam and ordered the rituals to stop immediately.

Selvam and his family were stunned. "What's the meaning of this?" Selvam demanded.

Raja's expression was stern. "What are you doing on my property?" he asked coldly.

Selvam frowned in confusion. "Sir, there must be some mistake. This land belongs to me. I purchased it recently and have all the necessary documents."

Raja remained unconvinced. He pulled out a set of papers and handed them to Selvam. "These are the documents for this land," Raja said. "I bought it for Rs. 6 crores, two days before your so-called purchase."

Selvam's hands trembled as he examined the papers. Everything appeared legitimate. His heart sank. It was clear that something was terribly wrong. Desperation overtook him as he tried to defend himself. "I know the broker who sold me this land!" he insisted, pulling out his phone to call Raghav. He dialed the number repeatedly, but each time, he was met with the same automated response: The number you are trying to reach is currently not available.

Raja, growing impatient, raised his voice. "I don't care about your excuses! You've got no right to be here. Get off my property immediately!"

Selvam's heart sank as the grim reality set in—he had been duped. The documents Raghav provided were clearly forged, and the land he thought was his was never his to begin with. Left with no other choice, Selvam reluctantly obeyed Raja's order and gathered his family to leave the site.

Anger and frustration boiled within him as he stormed over to Raghav's house later that day, hoping for answers. But when he arrived, the house was locked. He knocked furiously on the door, shouting Raghav's name, but there was no response.

A neighbor emerged, watching Selvam with a look of pity. "Raghav left a few days ago," the neighbor said. "He didn't tell anyone where he was going."

Selvam's fists clenched. He felt utterly helpless. Not knowing what else to do, he went to the police and filed a complaint. However, days passed, and there was no progress. The police couldn't track Raghav down. It was as if he had vanished into thin air.

Selvam's fury turned into despair. He had lost a significant portion of the money he had borrowed, and with it, the foundation of his dream was crumbling.

A few days later, Gopal decided to pay Selvam a visit to check on how he was progressing with the mall project. As they sat in the living room, Gopal casually asked, "So, Selvam, how's the new venture coming along? How have you put my money to use?"

Selvam's face turned pale. Hesitating, he eventually confessed, explaining how he had been scammed by the broker and lost the money he had invested in the land.

Gopal's demeanor shifted instantly. His eyes narrowed, and his voice rose in anger. "You did what? I trusted you, Selvam! That's the only reason I lent you such a large sum. And now, you're telling me you've lost it all?" He stood up abruptly, his face red with fury. "You're standing here looking like a complete fool!"

"I'm so sorry, Gopal. It's entirely my fault," Selvam said, his voice trembling. "I should have been more careful."

Gopal shook his head in disbelief, his hands clenched into fists. "I made a huge mistake trusting you. I don't care what you have to do, but I need my money back—and fast. If you don't pay me back soon, you'll regret it."

Without waiting for a response, Gopal stormed out of the house, slamming the door behind him. Selvam stood frozen, his head bowed, consumed by guilt and the overwhelming pressure of his predicament.

Selvam was also astounded by Gopal's reaction. He had always thought of Gopal as a close friend, someone who would stand by him in difficult times. But now, it was clear that Gopal valued his money far more than their friendship. The harsh reality stung— when it came to finances, Gopal's concern for their relationship seemed to vanish entirely.

Determined to avoid any further fallout, Selvam resolved to repay Gopal as quickly as possible. He couldn't risk Gopal taking drastic measures or tarnishing his family's reputation. The weight of the debt loomed over him like a storm cloud, and he knew that finding a solution would require immense effort and sacrifice.

Desperate to begin repaying his debt, Selvam made the difficult decision to sell Nirmala's jewelry. Although the money he received was far from sufficient, he hoped it would at least allow him to start repaying Gopal in small installments. Every rupee counted now.

However, the profits from his grocery store were meager, barely enough to cover his family's daily expenses, let alone chip away at the massive debt. Despite this, Selvam persisted, pouring his energy into the store, hoping to increase his earnings over time.

He meticulously saved every bit of profit, setting it aside with the singular goal of paying off Gopal. Though the road ahead was daunting, Selvam clung to the hope that his steady efforts, however small, would eventually bring him closer to clearing the debt and restoring his peace of mind.

One day, Gopal arrived at Selvam's house, flanked by two burly henchmen. His expression was cold and menacing as he stepped inside. Selvam, already on edge, quickly handed over the money he had managed to gather from selling Nirmala's jewelry and the profits from his grocery store.

Gopal counted the cash with a look of disdain. "Is this all?" he snapped. "When are you planning to pay the rest of the money? After my death?"

Selvam's voice was shaky but firm. "Gopal, I'm doing everything I can. The grocery store is my only source of income. I just need more time."

Gopal's patience snapped. He unleashed a torrent of derogatory language, insulting Selvam and his family. Nirmala and Swathi, who stood silently nearby, felt the sting of his harsh words.

Unable to tolerate the humiliation, Selvam's anger boiled over. He lunged forward, grabbing Gopal by the collar. "You can insult me, but don't you dare disrespect my family!" he shouted.

Before Selvam could do more, Gopal's henchmen intervened, shoving him backward. Gopal smirked and adjusted his shirt. "You've got a lot of nerve, Selvam," he said coldly. "I'll give you one month. If you don't pay the remaining amount by then, you and your family will regret it."

With that, Gopal stormed out, his thugs following close behind. The door slammed shut, leaving Selvam and his family in a tense, suffocating silence.

Selvam slumped into a chair, his head in his hands. The weight of the debt and Gopal's threats crushed him. After hours of agonizing thought, he reached a painful decision. "There's no other way," he concluded.

"I'll sell the house and the grocery shop," Selvam said, his voice heavy with resignation.

Nirmala's eyes widened in shock. "Are you out of your mind, Selvam? This is our home! The shop is our livelihood!" she protested.

"I know, Nirmala," Selvam replied, his voice trembling. "But if we don't do this, Gopal will destroy us. We'll find another way to rebuild our lives, but first, we need to get out from under this debt."

After a long, tearful discussion, Nirmala reluctantly agreed, understanding the gravity of their situation. Selvam began making arrangements, determined to salvage what little hope they had left.

Selvam sold both the house and the grocery shop, gathering just enough money to settle his debt with Gopal. Once the payment was made, Selvam felt a brief sense of relief, but it quickly dissolved as the harsh reality set in—his family was now homeless.

With nowhere to go, they found themselves on the streets, their belongings reduced to a few bags. The sight of his family huddled together on a footpath near a temple shattered Selvam. He was consumed by guilt, believing he alone was responsible for their downfall. The once-hopeful dreams of building a better future had turned into a daily struggle for survival.

Selvam and Nirmala began searching desperately for jobs. Any opportunity, no matter how small, was now a lifeline. Meanwhile, Vasudev and Swathi, unable to afford their school fees, had to drop out of school. Their education—once a beacon of hope—was suddenly out of reach.

When hunger struck, the family would go to the nearby temple, waiting in line for prasad. The simple offering became their only source of sustenance on many days. Nights were spent on the cold, hard pavement, with only the faint glow of the temple lights offering a semblance of security.

Despite the dire circumstances, Selvam clung to the hope that they could rise again. But each passing day on the streets deepened his resolve to find a way to rebuild their shattered lives.

One fateful night, as Selvam and his family lay sleeping on the footpath, the peace was shattered by the roar of a speeding car. The vehicle swerved uncontrollably, its driver too drunk to steer properly. In a horrific instant, the car veered onto the footpath, running over Swathi and Selvam before crashing into an electric pole with a deafening crash.

The impact jolted Vasudev and Nirmala awake. The chaos around them came into focus as they heard Selvam's anguished cries. Swathi lay nearby, eerily still, her fragile form unmoving. Nirmala's eyes filled with terror as she took in the scene. Seeing her husband writhing in pain and her daughter lifeless, she collapsed to her knees, sobbing uncontrollably.

Vasudev, shaken but determined, rushed to a nearby coin-operated public phone booth. His hands trembled as he dialed emergency medical services, his heart pounding with every second that passed.

Within minutes, an ambulance arrived, its siren cutting through the night. Paramedics quickly assessed the situation, placing Selvam, Swathi and the car driver on stretchers. The urgency in their movements only deepened the family's dread. Vasudev and Nirmala followed the ambulance to the hospital, clinging to hope amid the growing fear of what lay ahead.

At the government hospital, Selvam, Swathi, and the car driver were rushed into the emergency ward. The chaotic sounds of medical staff echoed in the background as Vasudev and Nirmala anxiously waited for news.

After what felt like an eternity, a doctor emerged, his face somber. "Selvam has sustained a broken back and a severely damaged leg. He is stable, but it will take him years of treatment and rehabilitation to walk again like a normal person," the doctor explained.

Relief flickered momentarily in Nirmala's eyes, but the doctor's next words hit like a thunderbolt. "I'm sorry," he said gently. "We couldn't save Swathi or the car driver. They were pronounced dead on arrival."

Nirmala let out a heart-wrenching wail, collapsing onto the floor as tears poured down her face. Vasudev, standing numbly beside her, couldn't take his eyes off Swathi's lifeless form, draped in a white sheet. His mind raced through memories of her laughter, her constant support, and the bond they shared. It felt unreal—a cruel nightmare he couldn't wake up from.

Grief overwhelmed him, and he staggered toward his sister's body. "Swathi…" he whispered, his voice breaking as he gently touched her cold hand. The weight of her loss crushed him, leaving him in a state of silent shock. Nirmala clung to him, sobbing uncontrollably, as they both mourned the irreparable void in their lives.

A few months after beginning his recovery, Selvam managed to secure a job as a cashier in a local supermarket. Though he still relied on a walking stick, he was determined to contribute to his family's livelihood. Nirmala, equally resolute, joined him at the same store as a salesperson. Their combined earnings, though modest, were enough to allow the family to move out of the streets and into a small rented house. It wasn't much, but it was a place they could call home—a sanctuary where they could start rebuilding their lives.

Recognizing Selvam's talent and dedication, the owner of the supermarket quickly saw his potential and, within two years, promoted him to regional manager. With this promotion, Selvam's income grew significantly, and the family's circumstances improved further. His career progression enabled them to move out of their rented house and purchase a larger, more comfortable home of their own—a monumental step in their journey of recovery.

Meanwhile, Vasudev returned to his studies, channelling his grief into academic pursuits. Education became his escape, a beacon of hope for a better future.

Though the loss of Swathi left an unfillable void, the family found solace in their resilience, leaning on one another as they worked toward a brighter tomorrow. Piece by piece, they stitched their lives back together, proving that even in the face of immense hardship, hope and determination could pave the way to normalcy.

Vasudev grew up with the weight of his family's hardships etched deeply into his heart. The tragic loss of his beloved sister, Swathi, continued to haunt him. Her death, he believed, was a direct result of the debt that had plunged his family into despair.

If not for that financial burden, their lives might have been different, happier.

As a child, Vasudev had been powerless, a mere spectator to his family's suffering. But as he matured, a burning desire took root within him—a wish to undo the past and reclaim the happiness they had lost. His scientific mind refused to dismiss the idea as mere fantasy. "What if there was a way to go back?" he thought. "What if I could change everything?"

Driven by this obsession, Vasudev began immersing himself in the study of time travel. He spent countless hours in Chennai's central library, poring over books that delved into the subject. Most were works of fiction, filled with imaginative tales of time machines and paradoxes. Yet, among the fiction, he found a handful of books that explored theoretical concepts—scientific frameworks that hinted at the possibility of manipulating time.

Despite the skepticism of others, Vasudev clung to the hope that time travel could be more than just a fantasy. Each book he read, each theory he absorbed, fueled his determination. He was no longer just dreaming of a way to change the past; he was actively seeking it, convinced that one day he might rewrite his family's history and bring Swathi back.

Frustrated by the lack of progress in his search, Vasudev one day approached the librarian with a bold request. "Sir, I've read all the books available in the public area. May I have permission to explore the chamber where the old and abandoned books are kept?"

The librarian hesitated for a moment, then nodded. "There's a room on the top floor," he said, handing Vasudev a key. "Be careful. It's been years since anyone's gone up there."

Vasudev climbed the creaky staircase to the top floor, the air growing heavier with the scent of dust and mildew. He unlocked the door to find a dim, neglected room, its shelves lined with crumbling books and papers. Cobwebs clung to the corners, and layers of dust coated every surface. He quickly covered his nose and mouth with a handkerchief and began his search.

Many of the books were too damaged to identify, their covers missing or their pages fused together with age. Undeterred, Vasudev carefully sifted through the piles, determined to uncover anything of value.

After hours of searching, his fingers brushed against something unusual—a bundle of yellowed papers tied together with a thin thread. Curious, he untied the bundle and gently unfolded the first sheet. The faded title on the page read: "CHRONOVISOR by Ernetti."

His heart raced as he flipped through the fragile pages. The book wasn't just a manuscript; it was a detailed guide, filled with diagrams, equations, and instructions on how to construct a device capable of viewing past events. The images were rough sketches of machinery, and the text described a device designed to harness electromagnetic traces left by historical events.

Excited but cautious, Vasudev carefully gathered the bundle and slipped it into his bag. He knew he had stumbled upon something extraordinary—something that could change everything. Making sure no one noticed, he returned the key to the librarian and left the building, his mind buzzing with possibilities.

At home, Vasudev locked himself in his room and began studying the mysterious document, his excitement growing with every page. Could this be the breakthrough I've been searching for? he thought. His journey to alter the past had just taken a significant leap forward.

Vasudev's discovery of the Chronovisor manuscript ignited a deeper passion for understanding the science behind time manipulation. Determined to turn theory into reality, he delved into the study of theoretical physics. His days were spent poring over books on quantum mechanics, wormholes, and other complex concepts that could potentially explain time travel.

By his second year of study, Vasudev had already begun constructing a prototype of the machine based on Ernetti's designs. His house gradually transformed into a workshop, filled with circuits, diagrams, and mechanical parts. The project became his obsession, driving him to seek answers beyond the scope of traditional academia.

After graduating, Vasudev accepted a position as a lecturer at the same college. Teaching allowed him to stay close to the resources he needed while providing a steady income to fund his experiments. But even as he excelled in his role, his mind remained focused on his machine.

A year into his teaching career, Vasudev realized the constraints of balancing work and his passion. He made a bold decision: to resign from his position and dedicate himself entirely to his project. With no safety net, he knew the risks were high, but the dream of altering his past and reclaiming his sister's life outweighed any fears.

Snapping out of his reverie, Vasudev felt a renewed determination surging through him. The memories of his past—his family's hardships, his sister's tragic death, and his tireless efforts to build the time machine—ignited a fire within him.

"Perhaps I pushed the machine too far," he thought, clenching his fists. *"The overload must have damaged the processors. But failure is part of progress. I'll rebuild it, and this time, I'll be more careful."*

His resolve solidified with each passing second. He refused to let one setback define the years of work and hope he had poured into this project. He knew that Swathi's memory and his family's sacrifices were his driving force.

Taking a deep breath to steady himself, Vasudev stood up from the bench. The cool evening breeze brushed against his face, and he felt a sense of clarity. He looked toward the horizon, his heart pounding with renewed purpose.

Without another moment's hesitation, he turned and began walking back home, his mind already working on the improvements he needed to make. This wasn't the end—it was just another step in his journey to rewrite the past.

Vasudev arrived home, his mind still buzzing with thoughts about improving his time machine. He knocked on the door, expecting Anu to answer immediately. But there was no response.

He knocked again, harder this time. "Open the door. It's me, Vasudev," he called out.

After a few tense moments, the door creaked open. Anu stood there, her face pale and visibly tense. She avoided making direct eye contact.

"What happened? Is everything okay?" Vasudev asked, his brows furrowing in concern.

"Oh! Yes... yes, everything is fine," Anu replied hastily, her voice shaky. "Where did you go?"

"I went to Marina Park," Vasudev said, stepping inside. "I needed some time to think." He glanced at her again, sensing something was off, but decided not to press further.

Anu gave a nervous smile, quickly closing the door behind him as Vasudev walked into his room, still lost in his own thoughts.

Roy returned home around 5:30 p.m., exhausted from a long day at work. As he approached his front door, he noticed it was slightly ajar. A sense of unease crept over him. He pressed the calling bell, but there was no response. Pushing the door open, he stepped inside cautiously.

What he saw in the hall froze him in place.

A man dressed in black lay sprawled on the floor, motionless. A knife was beside him, glinting in the fading evening light. Although the floor was tiled in brown, the area around the man was stained deep red—a pool of blood had spread out from his head.

Roy's heart raced as his eyes darted around the room. Near the TV stand, he spotted Sakshi lying unresponsive. Her head was bleeding, and her hand gripped a wooden lamp stand as if she had used it to defend herself. Nearby, Geetha lay unconscious near the kitchen doorway.

"Sakshi!" Roy gasped, rushing to her side. His hands trembled as he gently shook her. "Sakshi, wake up! Please!"

But there was no response. Tears welled up in his eyes, his mind racing with fear and confusion. He glanced at Geetha, who appeared to be breathing but remained unconscious.

Roy pulled out his phone with shaking hands and dialed the police. In a frantic voice, he described the horrific scene, urging them to come quickly.

As he hung up, he knelt beside Sakshi again, hoping and praying she would wake up. The weight of the unfolding tragedy pressed heavily on his chest, leaving him desperate for answers.

An hour later, the police arrived at Roy's residence, accompanied by an ambulance. Inspector Varun, a seasoned officer with a keen eye for detail, entered the house and surveyed the grim scene. His gaze fell on the lifeless bodies of Sakshi and the unknown man, as well as the unconscious Geetha near the kitchen.

The paramedics quickly got to work. Two ward boys descended from the ambulance, carefully transferring each body onto stretchers. The doctor inside the ambulance examined them. Moments later, he confirmed the worst: both Sakshi and the unidentified man were dead. However, to Roy's relief, Geetha was still alive.

As the ambulance doors closed, Geetha stirred slightly, her eyes fluttering open. She stared at the doctor in confusion.

"Who am I? What am I doing here?" she asked weakly, her voice barely a whisper.

The doctor placed a reassuring hand on her shoulder. "Don't strain yourself. Just relax. You've been through a lot. Rest for now," he said gently, administering a mild sedative. Geetha's eyelids grew heavy, and she drifted back to sleep.

Meanwhile, Inspector Varun turned to Roy, who was visibly shaken, his eyes red from crying.

"Can you tell me who that man is?" Varun asked, pointing to the body in the ambulance.

Roy shook his head, his voice cracking as he spoke. "No, sir. I've never seen him before. But… I'm certain he's the one who killed my wife." His words trembled with grief and rage.

Varun nodded, jotting down notes. "We'll need to investigate further. I'll need you to stay available for questioning."

Roy nodded, his gaze fixed on the ground, his world unraveling as he tried to comprehend the horror that had unfolded in his home.

Inspector Varun, determined to gather as much information as possible, stepped back into the ambulance to question Geetha. He gently roused her, hoping she could recall anything about the incident.

"Do you remember what happened in the house?" Varun asked, his tone calm but firm.

Geetha's eyes flickered open, confusion clouding her face. She shook her head weakly. "I… I don't remember… anything," she mumbled.

The doctor intervened, his voice cautious. "Inspector, she's lost her memory due to the head injury. Pressing her now could worsen her condition. It's best to let her rest and question her later."

Varun nodded reluctantly. He stepped out of the ambulance and returned to the crime scene, where two forensic officers were meticulously collecting fingerprints, blood samples, and other possible evidence. The atmosphere was tense, every creak and rustle in the house amplifying the gravity of the situation.

Varun turned to Roy. "Does anyone live in that house behind the trees?" he asked, pointing to a neighboring property partially obscured by foliage.

"Yes, sir," Roy replied. "A couple moved in about a week ago."

Without wasting time, Varun made his way to Vasudev's house. He knocked firmly on the door, and after a moment, Vasudev opened it, his face showing a mix of curiosity and concern at the sight of a police officer.

"Inspector," Varun introduced himself, stepping into the house. "I need to ask you a few questions."

"Of course, sir," Vasudev replied, stepping aside to let him in.

"Are you new to this area?" Varun asked, scanning the room as he spoke.

"Yes, we're from Chennai," Vasudev said. "My wife and I came to Andaman recently. We've only been here for a week."

Inspector Varun continued his questioning with an unyielding stare. "Where is your wife?" he asked.

"She's in the bathroom," Vasudev replied, trying to maintain his composure.

Varun's tone grew more serious. "Roy's wife and an unidentified man were found dead at Roy's house. Do you have any knowledge of this incident?"

"What!" Vasudev exclaimed, his face paling. "When did this happen?"

Varun's eyes narrowed. "So, you're not aware of the murder. Where were you the entire day?"

"I was at home until noon," Vasudev explained. "After that, I went to Marina Park for some fresh air."

"And your wife?" Varun pressed.

"She was home all day," Vasudev said, his voice steady but uneasy.

Varun nodded slowly. "I'd like to question your wife. When will she be out of the bathroom?"

Vasudev frowned, caught off guard. "I… I'm not sure, Sir. How would I know?"

Varun's gaze lingered on him for a moment before stepping back. "All right. I'm leaving for now, but I'll be back. Make sure you both stay in town until this case is resolved." His tone was firm, leaving no room for negotiation. Without another word, he turned and left the house.

As the door closed behind Varun, Vasudev stood frozen, grappling with the shocking news of Sakshi's murder. He felt a deep urge to visit Roy and offer his condolences, but the memory of Roy's harsh words earlier that day stopped him. "*He's probably still upset with me,*" Vasudev thought, conflicted but ultimately deciding to stay home.

After some time, Anu emerged from the bathroom, only to find Vasudev waiting for her, his arms crossed.

"What were you doing in there for over an hour?" he asked, scrutinizing her. "You don't even look like you've had a bath."

Anu shot him a sharp look. "I can do whatever I want in the bathroom. Why are you bothering me?" she snapped, brushing past him. She entered the bedroom and locked the door behind her without further explanation.

Vasudev stood there, his suspicion deepening. "*She's definitely hiding something,*" he thought. The unusual behavior, combined with the timing of the recent events, made him uneasy.

Meanwhile, Inspector Varun returned to Roy's residence to gather more information. "Do you know anything else about Vasudev and his wife?" he asked.

Roy shook his head. "Not much, Inspector. I invited them over for tea once. We had a decent chat. Vasudev mentioned he's a physicist working on a project, and Anu is a housewife. From what I've observed, Vasudev rarely leaves the house and spends most of his time tinkering with his so-called time machine."

Varun nodded, taking notes and snapping pictures of the crime scene. "We'll need you for further questioning as the investigation progresses," he said before leaving.

After Varun's departure, Roy's thoughts turned to Vasudev and Anu. *"Why haven't they come over to offer their condolences or even check on us?"* he wondered. It struck him as odd and suspicious, especially considering how close their houses were.

To aid in the investigation, Varun refrained from releasing Sakshi's photograph publicly at Roy's request. However, he did circulate the photo of the unidentified man found dead at the scene. The news spread like wildfire, making headlines across local media and even appearing on popular internet news platforms.

As the story gained traction, speculation grew, and people across the city started piecing together fragments of information. The case quickly became the talk of the town, intensifying the pressure on Varun to solve the mystery.

9. A Suspicious Death

Next day, in Chennai

Inspector Naidu was enjoying his morning routine, sipping tea while flipping through the newspaper. As he browsed the pages, a headline caught his attention: Double Murder Shocks Andaman Residents. The article detailed the case and included a photograph of the unidentified man who was found dead.

Naidu's heart skipped a beat when he recognized the face in the photograph—it was Ragul, the prime suspect in a high-profile robbery case he had been investigating. Shocked, Naidu immediately composed an email to Inspector Varun, providing details about Ragul's identity and his criminal background.

After sending the email, Naidu made a quick call to Gopal, the victim of the robbery. "Gopal, you won't believe this," Naidu said. "The man who robbed your house has been found dead in Andaman."

"I saw the news on TV this morning," Gopal replied, his tone a mix of surprise and relief. "Finally, some closure. At least he won't be a threat to anyone anymore."

With the primary suspect confirmed dead, Naidu saw no reason to keep the robbery case open. He officially closed the file, marking an end to one of his lingering investigations. However, the peculiar circumstances of Ragul's death left Naidu with a lingering sense of unease, as if the story wasn't entirely over.

At the Aberdeen Police station, Andaman

Inspector Varun sat at his desk, his eyes scanning the detailed email from Inspector Naidu. The email laid out Ragul's criminal history, including his involvement in the robbery at Gopal's house. After reading through the records, Varun quickly connected the dots. "*Ragul must have been the one who robbed Ratnakar's residence as well,*" he thought.

However, the larger mystery remained unsolved. "*But how did Ragul and Sakshi end up dead? And who attacked Geetha?*" Varun pondered, leaning back in his chair. The crime scene had been puzzling, with no clear sequence of events to explain what had transpired.

Varun hypothesized that Ragul and Sakshi might have gotten into a violent altercation. Perhaps Ragul had broken into the house, and during a struggle, both he and Sakshi had inflicted fatal wounds on each other. Geetha, in her attempt to protect her daughter, could have been injured by Ragul before losing consciousness.

Despite these theories, Varun's gut told him there was more to the story. His suspicion lingered on Vasudev and Anu. Their behavior and the timing of their arrival in Andaman raised questions. However, without solid evidence, Varun knew he couldn't act on mere intuition.

He glanced at the clock. *"The forensic reports are due tomorrow evening,"* he reminded himself. They could hold the key to unraveling the truth behind this complex case. Until then, Varun decided to keep a close watch on Vasudev and Anu, ready to act the moment new evidence emerged.

Vasudev was deep into his work, tinkering with the time machine in his makeshift lab. His mind raced with possibilities. *"If I can boost the processor's capacity, maybe the machine will work without overloading,"* he thought. But the challenge was clear—he didn't have the funds to buy new components. Desperate, he disassembled his television, scavenging it for usable parts.

The room was filled with the soft hum of electronics, and Vasudev was so engrossed in his work that he barely noticed the time. Suddenly, a loud banging at the main door broke his concentration. The noise startled him, and for a moment, he hesitated.

"Who could it be at this hour?" he wondered as he made his way to the door.

He opened it to find Roy standing there, his face darkened with anger. His frown deepened as he locked eyes with Vasudev.

Roy's fury boiled over as he grabbed Vasudev by the collar. "What did you do to my wife? Why did you kill her?" he demanded, his voice trembling with rage and grief.

Vasudev was stunned. "Why are you holding me responsible for your wife's death?" he asked, his eyes wide with confusion.

Roy's grip tightened momentarily. "I *know* you're involved!" he shouted. "I can feel it—you or your wife had something to do with it."

"I swear to God, Mr. Roy, I didn't do anything," Vasudev pleaded. "Please, let go of my collar and allow me to explain."

Roy hesitated, his breath heavy, then slowly released Vasudev. The weight of his emotions overwhelmed him as he staggered into the house, slumping onto the couch. His anger gave way to sorrow, and tears streamed down his face.

"I'm sorry, Vasudev," Roy muttered between sobs. "I'm just… I'm lost. My wife is gone, and I don't know what to do."

Vasudev sat down across from him, his expression somber. "I completely understand what you're going through," he said softly. "I'm deeply saddened by your loss, Roy. Sakshi was a wonderful person."

The room fell into a heavy silence, broken only by Roy's quiet sobs. Vasudev knew that words alone couldn't heal Roy's pain.

Roy wiped his tears, his voice shaky but firm. "I feel like I've lost everything since my wife's death. And now, my mother-in-law has lost her memory and is in the hospital."

Vasudev placed a comforting hand on Roy's shoulder. "It's a terrible tragedy, Roy. But trust me, the police will find the culprit soon. Don't lose hope."

Roy looked up, his eyes searching Vasudev's face. "Vasudev, I need to ask you something. Will you give me an honest answer?"

"I have nothing to hide from you," Vasudev replied. "Ask me anything."

Roy leaned forward, his voice low and serious. "Where were you when my wife was murdered?"

Vasudev sighed, meeting Roy's gaze. "I was really upset when my time machine broke," he began. "It felt like years of hard work had gone to waste. So, I went to Marina Park to clear my head and escape my frustration. I didn't know anything about what had happened to Sakshi until I heard the news. I thought of coming to see you afterward, but since you were upset earlier that day, I decided to wait."

Roy nodded slowly, but his suspicions weren't entirely eased. "And what about your wife? What was she doing during that time?"

"She was here at home," Vasudev said. "She told me she didn't know anything about the incident either."

Roy's brows furrowed, deep in thought. "I see," he murmured. "I just hope the truth comes out soon."

"So do I," Vasudev said, his tone sincere. "I'm here if you need anything."

Roy rose from the couch, his movements slow and heavy. He walked toward the front door, pausing briefly before stepping out. "I have faith in you both," he said, his voice laced with pain. "Please, for God's sake, let me know if you learn anything about my wife's death." Without waiting for a reply, he left, his heart clearly shattered.

Vasudev stood by the door, watching Roy disappear into the night. The weight of their conversation lingered, filling the house with an oppressive silence. Vasudev felt a deep sadness, his mind racing with questions. *"What really happened to Sakshi?"* he thought. The urge to uncover the truth grew stronger. *"Maybe my machine can help,"* he reasoned. *"I could use it to see what happened that day."*

Driven by this thought, Vasudev went to check on Anu. As he entered the bedroom, he found her lying on the bed, her breathing steady but her posture unusually rigid. Something felt off. He approached her quietly. "Anu, are you feeling okay?" he asked softly.

Anu didn't stir, pretending to be in a deep sleep. Vasudev lingered for a moment, observing her, but chose not to press further. *"She must be exhausted,"* he concluded, though a nagging doubt lingered in the back of his mind.

Shaking off his unease, Vasudev turned and left the room. His focus shifted back to the time machine. *"I need to fix it,"* he thought, his resolve hardening. *"If it works, I can finally see what happened and help Roy find peace."* He headed back to his workspace, determined to make the necessary repairs.

10. The Accident

Roy was on his way to work, though his heart wasn't in it. He felt the heavy burden of responsibility toward his employees, yet his mind refused to let go of the grief. His thoughts drifted to Sakshi, replaying cherished moments they had shared. The road ahead blurred as his focus wavered, lost in memories.

Caught in this mental haze during the bustling rush hour, Roy's concentration slipped entirely. Without realizing it, he veered onto the wrong side of the road, crossing the divider. He was oblivious to the oncoming truck barreling toward him at high speed.

The blaring horn of the truck couldn't pierce the fog of his thoughts. A sudden, violent jolt shook his car, snapping him back to reality. Too late—he saw the truck just before impact. The collision was brutal. The force of the crash propelled Roy forward. His body smashed through the windshield, sending shards of glass flying as he was thrown onto the front of the truck.

Roy landed with a sickening thud, groaning in pain. His face was a mess of cuts, glass shards embedded deeply in his skin. Blood trickled from the gashes on his arms and legs, painting a grim picture of his injuries. Meanwhile, the truck driver escaped unscathed, stepping out to assess the damage.

A crowd quickly gathered, horrified by the scene. Bystanders rushed to Roy's aid, some calling for emergency services. Within minutes, an ambulance arrived, its siren wailing. The paramedics worked swiftly, carefully placing Roy on a stretcher and rushing him to the nearest government hospital.

As the ambulance sped away, the gravity of Roy's condition weighed heavily on everyone who had witnessed the accident.

Upon arrival at the hospital, Roy was swiftly taken to the X-ray department on a stretcher. The medical staff worked quickly, scanning his injuries to assess the extent of the damage. The results were grim—multiple fractures in his ribs and arms, along with severe lacerations.

Without delay, Roy was moved to the Intensive Care Unit (ICU), where a team of doctors prepared for emergency surgery. He was administered anesthesia, and the surgeons began their work, carefully addressing his fractured bones and deep wounds. The operation lasted for nearly an hour, during which the doctors stabilized his condition and ensured no internal bleeding.

Once the surgery was complete, Roy was transferred to a recovery ward. His head was heavily bandaged, leaving only his eyes, nose, and mouth exposed. His chest bore several stitches, and both of his arms were encased in plaster of Paris. Bandages wrapped tightly around his legs, covering the cuts and bruises sustained during the crash.

Still under the influence of anesthesia, Roy remained unconscious, his body resting as the hospital staff monitored his vital signs closely. The room was quiet, save for the steady beeping of the heart monitor, marking the start of his long road to recovery.

Roy slowly regained consciousness, blinking through the narrow slits left by the bandages on his face. The sterile scent of the hospital and the soft beeping of machines surrounded him. As his eyes adjusted, he noticed two familiar figures standing by his bedside—his closest friends. They had rushed over after hearing about the accident.

Seeing Roy's fragile state, tears welled up in their eyes. "We're here for you, Roy," one of them said softly. But the words offered little comfort. Roy couldn't hold back his own tears and began to sob quietly.

"Why did this happen?" Roy murmured, his voice barely audible. "I don't want to live... I want to be with Sakshi."

Before his friends could respond, Inspector Varun entered the ward, clipboard in hand. His expression was stern but professional. He had come to gather information for his investigation into the accident.

"How are you feeling, Roy?" Varun asked, his tone direct.

Roy struggled to speak through the bandages. "I don't want to live," he muttered again. "I want to be with my wife."

Varun's patience wore thin. "Stop talking rubbish and tell me what happened!" he demanded, his voice firm but not unkind.

Roy took a deep, shaky breath. "It was my fault," he admitted, his words slow and labored. "I wasn't paying attention. I was… lost in my thoughts. I drove onto the wrong side of the road and didn't see the truck until it was too late."

Varun nodded, jotting down notes on his clipboard. "You're lucky to be alive, Roy," he said. "But you need to focus on getting better. We'll handle the rest."

The questioning lasted a few more minutes, with Varun gathering all the necessary details. Once he was satisfied, he put away his notepad and stood up. "Take care of yourself, Roy," he said. "And let me know if you remember anything else."

"Did you find out who the murderer is?" Roy asked weakly, his voice tinged with both hope and despair.

Inspector Varun paused, looking at Roy with a firm expression. "No, not yet," he admitted. "But rest assured, whoever did this will be caught and severely punished." With that, Varun gave Roy a reassuring nod and left the ward.

A short while later, a doctor entered, carrying a small tray of medications. "How are you feeling, Mr. Roy?" the doctor asked, checking the monitors and adjusting Roy's IV.

Roy didn't respond, his thoughts still fixated on Sakshi and the mystery surrounding her death.

"These medications will help manage your pain and prevent infection," the doctor explained as he administered the medicine. "You've been through a lot, but with proper care, you'll recover."

Roy gave a slight nod, his eyes heavy with grief. The doctor finished his work and left him to rest. The ward fell silent once more, save for the rhythmic hum of the medical equipment, as Roy lay back, consumed by sorrow and a burning desire for justice.

In Vasudev's house.

The house was quiet, save for the faint hum of Vasudev's work in his makeshift lab. Suddenly, the sharp ring of a phone echoed through the hall room. Without looking up from his project, Vasudev called out, "Anu, can you get that?"

No response. She was still in the bathroom. Sighing, Vasudev set down his tools and walked to the hall, picking up the phone.

"Hello?" he said, already guessing who it might be.

"Hello, Vasu. How are you?" Nirmala's familiar voice greeted him, warm yet tinged with concern.

Vasudev paused briefly, guilt creeping in. "I'm fine, Ma. How are you? How's Papa?"

"We're both fine," Nirmala replied, her voice soft but slightly reproachful. "I was worried. You haven't called in so long."

"I'm sorry, Ma," Vasudev said, his tone apologetic. "I've been swamped with work. I didn't mean to worry you."

Nirmala sighed but didn't press further. "How's Anu? Are you taking good care of her?"

"Of course, Ma," Vasudev assured her. "But I'm a little concerned. She's been acting a bit off these past few days."

"Don't overthink it," Nirmala said gently. "She's in a new place. It takes time to adjust. Just be patient with her." After a brief pause, she added, "So, tell me, have you two visited any interesting places in Andaman?"

Vasudev rubbed the back of his neck. "Not yet. We're still deciding. In the meantime, I've been focusing on my project."

Nirmala's tone shifted, becoming more insistent. "Vasu, remember why you're there. This isn't just about work. It's a chance for you and Anu to spend quality time together. Set your project aside for a bit, enjoy the island, and come back with good news." Her voice softened. "Keep each other happy, Vasu. That's what matters."

A small smile tugged at Vasudev's lips. "Hmm… sure, Ma. I'll keep that in mind."

There was a brief rustling on the other end before Nirmala spoke again. "Wait, your father wants to talk to you."

A moment later, Selvam's familiar voice came through the line. "Hello, Vasu! Don't tell me you've forgotten about your old man." His chuckle was light, but it carried the warmth of familiarity.

Vasudev chuckled back. "Stop it, Appa. Of course, I haven't. How are you?"

"I'm fine," Selvam replied. "Do you know your mother's birthday is next week?"

"Yes, I do," Vasudev said with a grin. "I've got a surprise planned for her."

"Oh? What is it?" Selvam asked, curiosity piqued. "I'll keep it a secret, I promise."

"It's a bit complicated," Vasudev replied, laughing lightly. "You wouldn't understand, Appa."

Selvam laughed. "Fair enough, Vasu. But don't forget to call her on the day."

"Don't worry, I won't," Vasudev assured him. "I'll talk to you later, Appa. I've got some important work to finish."

"Alright, Vasu. Take care."

With that, Vasudev hung up. He stood still for a moment, the warmth of the call lingering in the quiet house. Then, taking a deep breath, he turned back to his project, the weight of his mother's words still fresh in his mind.

11. The Reports

When Varun returned to the police station that evening, he found a stack of files neatly placed on his desk. A constable approached him and said, "Sir, these are the autopsy reports you requested."

Varun nodded, picked up the top file, and began flipping through the pages. The details were both revealing and puzzling. The fingerprints collected from the crime scene belonged to three individuals: Sakshi, Ragul, and Geetha. He read further, focusing on the cause of death for the victims.

Both Sakshi and Ragul had died from severe head trauma. However, as he reviewed the timeline of their deaths, something didn't sit right. The autopsy report indicated that Sakshi had died before Ragul.

Varun's brows furrowed. *"If Sakshi died before Ragul, who killed Ragul?"* he thought, the puzzle growing more complex. He leaned back in his chair, his mind racing with possibilities.

"Could Geetha have killed Ragul?" he murmured to himself. The idea seemed plausible, but Geetha's apparent memory loss complicated matters. *"Is she pretending to have memory loss to cover up her actions?"* he wondered.

Another possibility gnawed at him—"Could there have been a fourth person at the crime scene, someone clever enough to erase their fingerprints and leave no trace?"

Varun closed the file and stared at his desk, his instincts telling him there was more to the story than what the reports revealed. He made a mental note to revisit Geetha for further questioning and to explore any potential leads regarding a possible unknown individual at the scene. The pieces of the puzzle were slowly falling into place, but the picture they formed was far from clear.

Varun leaned back in his chair, the autopsy report still open in front of him. His mind was abuzz with possibilities. "If Geetha isn't faking her memory loss, then someone else must have been at the scene—a fourth person who managed to erase their presence. But who? And why would they murder Ragul after Sakshi?"

The unanswered questions swirled in his head like a storm, each one pulling him deeper into the mystery. His thoughts were interrupted by the sharp ring of the landline phone on his desk. He picked up the receiver.

"Hello," he said, his tone sharp but composed.

After sometime, Varun placed the receiver down abruptly, his mind racing with the new revelation. The possibility of a fourth person at the crime scene had gone from a theory to a reality. He stood up, grabbed his notepad, and barked an order to a nearby constable.

"Get two men ready immediately. We're heading out," he said with urgency.

Within minutes, two constables joined him, their expressions alert. Without wasting time, Varun climbed into his jeep, the constables following suit. The engine roared to life as Varun drove with determination, his destination clear—Vasudev's residence.

Upon reaching Vasudev's residence, Varun knocked the main door aggressively. His aggressive knocks echoed through the quiet neighborhood as he shouted, "Vasudev! Open the door. It's Inspector Varun!"

The house remained eerily silent, save for faint, indistinct noises coming from inside. Varun's suspicion grew. *"He's in there,"* Varun thought. *"Why isn't he opening the door?"* His frustration mounted as he continued pounding on the door, his voice growing louder with each call. But Vasudev didn't respond.

Fury flickered in Varun's eyes. "He's avoiding us," he muttered under his breath. Turning to the constables, he barked, "Break it down!"

The constables nodded and charged at the door. Their boots struck the wood repeatedly, each kick growing more forceful. The sound of splintering echoed with each impact until finally, with one final blow, the door gave way. The lock broke, and the door swung open, revealing the interior of Vasudev's home.

Varun and his team stormed inside, their eyes scanning every corner of the house. "Search the premises!" Varun ordered sharply.

They moved quickly through the rooms. In one of them, they found Vasudev sitting on a chair, his focus fixed on a large computer-like machine in front of him. The hum of the device filled the room, but Vasudev's expression was eerily calm, almost detached.

"Vasudev!" Varun shouted, his voice slicing through the tension. Vasudev didn't flinch. His fingers hovered over the keyboard, as if he were lost in his work.

Varun's eyes darted to a corner of the room, and his breath caught in his throat. His stomach turned as he took in the horrifying sight.

Anu lay lifeless in a pool of blood, her wide-open eyes staring into nothingness. Her back was propped against the wall, and her pale face bore a frozen expression of terror. A blood-smeared knife rested on the floor in front of her, its metallic sheen glinting in the dim light.

Varun's rage boiled over as he trained his pistol squarely on Vasudev. "What have you done?" he barked, his voice echoing in the tense room.

Vasudev remained silent, his demeanor calm and unsettling. Blood smeared his hands, and his focus was locked on the machine in front of him. He adjusted a strap on his wrist, securing what appeared to be a watch-like device. The machine's viewer flickered, displaying the text: "Processing 85%."

"Don't ignore me!" Varun roared, his finger tightening on the trigger. "You're under arrest!"

Vasudev turned slowly, his eyes meeting Varun's with unnerving composure. A faint smile played on his lips, sending a chill through the room.

"Surrender yourself, Vasudev!" Varun demanded, his voice laced with fury and disbelief. "I know you killed Sakshi and Ragul! And now, you've murdered your own wife!"

Vasudev's smile didn't waver, and his silence was deafening. His unflinching gaze locked with Varun's, as if daring him to act. The room grew thick with tension, the hum of the machine and the faint ticking of the watch-like device the only sounds cutting through the silence.

Varun's grip on the pistol tightened further, his mind racing. *What kind of man smiles in the face of such accusations?* He felt the weight of the moment pressing down on him, the answers he sought slipping further out of reach.

The hum of the machine abruptly ceased, and an eerie silence filled the room. The viewer on the machine displayed the words: "Processing complete." At the same moment, the watch-like device on Vasudev's wrist began glowing a vivid blue, casting an ethereal light across the dimly lit room.

Varun's grip on his pistol tightened as his nerves frayed. "What are you doing?" he demanded, his voice a mixture of anger and unease.

Vasudev remained calm, his movements deliberate. He slowly extended his left hand toward a button on the computer.

"Stop! Raise both of your hands and surrender!" Varun yelled, his finger poised on the trigger.

Vasudev paused momentarily, locking eyes with Varun. A faint, enigmatic smile appeared on his face. "It's too late, Varun," he said, his voice unnervingly composed.

Before Varun could react, Vasudev pressed the button. Instantly, a dazzling white light erupted from the device on his wrist, enveloping him in a cascade of electricity. Sparks crackled and danced around his body as he was lifted from the chair, suspended in mid-air. The constables froze in shock, their eyes wide with disbelief.

"What the…?" Varun muttered, struggling to comprehend the surreal sight before him. Fear and instinct took over. He raised his pistol and pulled the trigger.

The gunshot echoed in the room, but before the bullet could reach Vasudev, there was a blinding flash of light. The entire room was illuminated in an instant, forcing everyone to shield their eyes. When the light faded, Vasudev was gone.

Varun stared in disbelief at the empty space where Vasudev had been just moments ago. The bullet had lodged harmlessly into the wall behind the chair. The constables exchanged bewildered glances, unable to process what had just transpired.

"Where did he go?" one of them whispered, his voice trembling.

Varun lowered his gun, his hands shaking slightly. "I… I don't know," he said, his mind racing. "But whatever just happened… this is far from over."

12. Mending the Past

The world around Vasudev was quiet, almost eerily so, as his senses slowly returned to him. He felt disoriented but gradually became aware of faint sounds—distant voices, the rustling of fabric, and the creak of wooden beams. His body ached, but the silence was broken by a sneeze, the dusty air irritating his nose.

He opened his eyes cautiously, his vision adjusting to the dimly lit room. It was small and filled with old rugs, brass lamps, and decorative items that seemed untouched for years. Dust clung to every surface, giving the room an ancient, forgotten feel.

Pushing himself up slowly, Vasudev's mind raced. *"Where am I?"*

He strained his ears and heard the hum of activity outside. He spotted a shawl draped over a chair in the corner and instinctively grabbed it, wrapping it around his head and shoulders to conceal his face. Quietly, he slipped out of the room, his footsteps muffled by the dusty floor.

Outside, the scene was lively yet oddly familiar. He observed the surroundings carefully—the vibrant temple walls adorned with intricate carvings, the flickering flames of oil lamps, and garlands of marigolds hanging from every corner. A wave of realization washed over him. *"This is the temple where my marriage ceremony was supposed to happen."*

His heart raced as he tried to comprehend what was happening. He caught sight of a priest walking by, holding a silver plate with flowers and incense. Vasudev's hands, still stained with dried blood, were hastily shoved into his pant pockets to avoid drawing attention.

Summoning his composure, he approached the priest cautiously. "Swamiji," he said, his voice low and muffled by the shawl. "Is there any marriage ceremony scheduled to take place here today?"

"Oh yes," the priest replied. "Are you asking about Vasudev and Anu's marriage?"

Vasudev's heart skipped a beat when the priest mentioned his name. He stood frozen for a moment, processing the confirmation of his suspicions. *"The machine worked perfectly,"* he thought, a mix of excitement and dread washing over him. He had truly traveled back to the day of his wedding—the pivotal moment he had long sought to change.

He quickly composed himself, adjusting the shawl to ensure his face remained hidden. "Yes, Swamiji," he replied softly, masking the trembling in his voice.

The priest smiled kindly. "You've arrived a little early for the ceremony. The groom's family has yet to arrive, but the bride's family is already here. They are making final preparations."

Vasudev nodded, his thoughts racing. *The bride's family… Anu is here."* The name sent a shiver down his spine, stirring memories of betrayal, fear, and everything he had worked tirelessly to escape.

"Thank you, Swamiji," he said, bowing slightly. "I'll wait nearby."

The priest gave him a curious look but shrugged and continued on his way, disappearing down the temple corridor.

Vasudev stepped back into the shadows, his mind whirling with conflicting emotions. "Anu and her family are here. The ceremony hasn't started yet. That means I still have time."

Clenching his fists in his pockets, he resolved to stay unnoticed and observe. He needed to ensure the sequence of events unfolded as he remembered—or to make the changes that would alter his fate. One thing was certain: his mission had begun.

Dressed as a priest with the help of some clothes found in the store room, his face obscured by a scarf, Vasudev walked through the marriage hall with cautious steps. The vibrant scene was surreal—guests chatting, relatives arranging flowers, and children running around—all unaware of the storm brewing within him. *"I must remain unnoticed,"* he thought, scanning the hall for his target.

Spotting the path to the bride's room behind the dais, he moved discreetly, careful not to draw attention. The muffled hum of activity behind the closed door confirmed that Anu and her family were inside. Summoning his courage, Vasudev knocked softly.

The door creaked open, revealing Neerja, Anu's mother, her expression polite but questioning as she looked at him. "Yes, what is it, Swamiji?" she asked, her tone brisk but kind.

Vasudev bowed slightly, his voice muffled beneath the scarf. "Namaste. I am here to perform a brief blessing for the bride before the ceremony. It's part of an old custom," he lied, keeping his tone low and reverent.

Neerja hesitated for a moment, her gaze narrowing slightly. "A blessing? That's unusual… but I suppose there's no harm. Please, wait here. I'll check with Anu."

She stepped back into the room, leaving the door ajar. Vasudev could hear the faint jingling of bangles and the murmur of voices as Anu prepared inside. His heart pounded in his chest. *"This is it. I'm so close."*

Moments later, Neerja returned, her face still uncertain but willing. "All right. Please be quick. The ceremony is about to begin."

Vasudev nodded, stepping into the room. His eyes met Anu's for the briefest of moments before he quickly averted his gaze, pretending to adjust his scarf. *"Stay calm. Stay focused,"* he reminded himself.

The room was filled with ornate decorations, jewelry boxes, and the soft scent of flowers. Anu sat on a low stool, adjusting her veil, her expression a mix of nervousness and detachment. Vasudev took a deep breath, ready to execute the plan forming in his mind.

The room was filled with a thick tension as Vasudev revealed his blood-stained hands and stood menacingly, his face partially obscured by the scarf, his blood-stained hands making Neerja and Anu tremble in terror.

"What are you doing, Swamiji? What exactly do you want?" Neerja stammered, her voice quivering with fear.

"Sssshhhh…. Keep quiet, or I'll kill you both," Vasudev hissed, deliberately altering his voice to ensure they wouldn't recognize him. His tone was cold, devoid of emotion.

Anu's sobs broke the silence as tears streamed down her face. She clung to her mother, trembling uncontrollably. The sight only hardened Vasudev's resolve. He pointed to the glowing device strapped to his wrist. "Look at this," he said, his voice growing more intense. "This is a remote button for a bomb I've planted somewhere in the hall. If you want to save everyone's life, you'll do as I say. Stop this marriage, or I'll blow this place to pieces."

"Why are you doing this?" Neerja managed to ask, her voice cracking under the weight of fear.

"That doesn't matter," Vasudev barked. "What matters is your life and the lives of everyone in that hall." His tone was sharp, cutting through their protests.

Anu tried to speak, but her voice faltered. She could barely form words. "Who are you?" she whispered through her sobs.

"It doesn't matter who I am," Vasudev replied. "All you need to know is that I have no qualms about killing everyone here if you don't do exactly what I say."

He took a step closer, looming over them. "If you try to alert anyone—your father, the guests, or the police—I'll press this button on my watch, and this will be your final day on earth. Do you understand?"

Neerja nodded, her lips trembling, while Anu stared at him in utter disbelief, tears streaking her face.

"Good," Vasudev said with an edge of finality. "Now, when the time comes, you'll find a way to call off this wedding. No excuses, no delays. If I sense even a hint of resistance…" He glanced pointedly at the device on his wrist.

The room fell into an oppressive silence, punctuated only by Anu's stifled sobs. Vasudev knew his actions were drastic, but his resolve was unwavering. He couldn't let the events of this day repeat themselves, not this time.

Anu's sobs grew louder as she clung to her mother. "Please… please spare our lives. We promise not to tell anyone," she said, her voice trembling. "I'll do what you said. I'll stop the wedding."

Vasudev stared at her for a moment, his expression cold and unreadable. "Good. Then stop crying!" he barked. "Remember, if this marriage isn't stopped… BOOM!"

His voice carried a menacing finality as he pointed to the device on his wrist one last time. Without another word, he turned and walked toward the door, opening it just enough to slip out without drawing attention.

Neerja and Anu were left in the room, paralyzed with fear, their minds racing. They knew they had no choice but to comply with the stranger's chilling demands.

Anu wiped her tears, her heart pounding. The weight of the threat hung heavy in the air, and the sound of Vasudev's retreating footsteps echoed ominously in their ears.

Vasudev's heart raced as he sat on a chair near the entrance, his eyes fixed on the marriage dais. *"I hope the plan works,"* he thought nervously. Every second felt like an eternity as he anxiously watched the activity in the hall.

Suddenly, the arrival of a group of people caught his attention. He froze, his eyes widening in shock. Leading the group was none other than himself—Vasudev from the past—accompanied by his family. His younger self looked calm and composed, a stark contrast to the turmoil Vasudev (from the future) was feeling.

"This is surreal," he thought. Seeing his past self was both disorienting and unsettling. *"So, this is how it begins."*

Vasudev (from the past) greeted a few relatives and exchanged pleasantries before heading toward the groom's room, which was located behind the marriage dais. His mother followed him, a warm smile on her face.

Vasudev (from the future) clenched his fists. "I need to stay focused. I can't let my emotions get in the way."

As his past self disappeared behind the dais, Vasudev leaned back slightly in his chair, keeping a low profile. He pulled the scarf tighter around his face, ensuring no one would recognize him. The sight of his younger self brought back a flood of memories.

"This is my chance to stop it all," he thought, steeling himself.

After a few minutes, Vasudev (from the future) watched intently as his past self emerged from the groom's room, accompanied by his mother. His heart sank as he saw the calm expressions on their faces, unaware of the chaos that was about to unfold. Vasudev (from the past) stepped onto the dais, settling into his designated spot with a serene demeanor, while his mother sat nearby, pride shining in her eyes.

Moments later, the priest performing the ceremony raised his hand to summon the bride. All eyes turned toward the bride's room as Anu emerged, her head slightly bowed, her hand held by her mother, Neerja. Her ornate bridal attire shimmered in the temple's warm light, but her face betrayed her fear. Her eyes darted nervously around the hall as she was led to the dais.

Anu sat beside Vasudev (from the past), her movements stiff and hesitant. She seemed disconnected, as if struggling to contain an internal storm.

The priest began reciting mantras, his voice resonating through the hall. He sprinkled holy water and threw twigs into the sacred flame, the fire crackling and sending smoke spiraling upward. The scent of burning herbs filled the air.

From his vantage point, Vasudev (from the future) noticed Anu's trembling hands as she adjusted her bridal bangles. Her terror was evident, her face pale despite the colorful decorations adorning her. *"She's scared,"* Vasudev (from the future) thought. *"This is the moment."*

As the priest continued chanting, Vasudev's (from the future) mind raced. *"Anu, don't wait too long. You have to act now, before it's too late."* He gripped the edge of his chair, his concealed presence shrouded in both anticipation and apprehension.

The atmosphere in the hall grew tense as the wedding rituals approached their climax. Just as Vasudev (from the past) reached for the *mangalsutra* to tie around Anu's neck, her voice rang out sharply, cutting through the priest's chants.

"Stop!" she said, her voice loud and resolute.

The entire hall fell silent, the guests stunned by her sudden outburst. All eyes turned toward her in shock.

"I am not interested in this marriage," Anu declared, her voice trembling but firm.

Gasps rippled through the crowd. Prabhu, Anu's father, looked bewildered and furious. "What are you saying, Anu? Why are you doing this at the last moment?" he demanded.

"I agreed to this marriage only because you both forced me," Anu said, her tone defiant as she gestured toward her parents. "I don't like Vasudev."

"Enough, Anu! Stop this nonsense!" Prabhu yelled, his face flushed with anger. He raised his hand to slap her, but Neerja stepped forward and grabbed his arm.

"Let her go," Neerja said, her voice a mix of panic and sadness.

Anu didn't wait for anyone to stop her. She stood up abruptly, descended from the dais, and ran out of the hall, tears streaming down her face. Neerja followed her, calling out her name.

The hall was left in chaos. Vasudev's parents sat frozen, their expressions a mix of humiliation and heartbreak. Vasudev (from the past) quickly rose, trying to console them as the guests began to murmur and disperse. One by one, they quietly left the hall, leaving an air of discomfort and confusion behind.

In a corner, Vasudev (from the future) watched the scene unfold. A sense of triumph welled within him. *"The mission is accomplished,"* he thought. *"I've stopped the wedding."*

Satisfied, he rose from his seat and made his way out of the hall, blending in with the departing guests. As he walked away, he noticed Neerja standing outside the hall, wiping her tears. Her attention shifted to him, and something about his demeanor caught her eye. Curiosity and suspicion flickered across her face.

Unbeknownst to Vasudev, Neerja began following him at a safe distance. He headed toward the storeroom where he had hidden earlier. Neerja trailed him, careful not to draw attention to herself.

Vasudev entered the storeroom, shutting the door behind him. Neerja saw her chance. She approached the door cautiously, ready to lock him inside and notify the authorities. But as she reached for the door, a sudden, dazzling flash of light seeped out from beneath it, momentarily blinding her.

Startled, she hesitated for a moment before pushing the door open. The room was empty. There was no sign of Vasudev, nor were there any windows or other means of escape.

Neerja stood in the doorway, bewildered. Her heart raced as she looked around the room. "Where did he go?" she whispered to herself, unable to comprehend the mystery that had just unfolded before her.

13. The Consequences

Vasudev jolted back to the present day. He was at his home in Andaman. The air was heavy with silence, an eerie stillness settling over the room. As he looked around, he realized something was different. He was alone. The corner of the room where Anu's lifeless body had been was now empty. Even the bloodstains that had smeared his hands earlier were gone.

"The machine worked!" Vasudev whispered to himself, his voice trembling with a mix of disbelief and elation. A surge of joy coursed through him. *"I did it. I changed the past."*

But his triumph was short-lived. A sharp knocking at the main door startled him. He froze, his heart pounding in his chest. The knocking persisted, louder this time. Taking cautious steps, he approached the door, his mind racing. *"Who could it be?"*

As he opened the door, his breath caught. Standing before him was Sakshi, alive and well.

"You!" Vasudev exclaimed, his eyes wide with shock. His mind reeled. *"Sakshi was dead. How is she standing here?"*

Sakshi tilted her head, her brows furrowing. "Why? What happened? Were you expecting someone else?" she asked, her tone laced with curiosity.

"Uh… no," Vasudev stammered, forcing himself to speak. His voice trembled slightly.

"I just came by to invite you for tea later this evening," Sakshi said, her expression softening into a smile.

"Oh… uh… sure. I'd be delighted to join you," Vasudev replied, managing a weak smile, though his mind was spinning.

"Great! See you then," Sakshi said cheerfully before turning and heading back to her house.

Vasudev shut the door slowly, leaning against it as confusion overwhelmed him. *"What just happened?"* He dropped onto the couch, his thoughts a whirlwind. *"Was that really Sakshi? Am I hallucinating? Or has something truly changed because of my journey through time?"*

The enormity of what had transpired weighed heavily on him. He had succeeded in altering the past, but the consequences were beginning to surface, unraveling reality around him in unexpected ways.

Exhausted from the mental and physical toll of time travel, Vasudev decided he needed rest. He retreated to his bedroom, his mind still grappling with the inexplicable, and lay down.

Within moments, he succumbed to sleep, his dreams clouded by the mysteries of his altered world.

As evening settled in, Vasudev made his way to Sakshi's house. Geetha, Sakshi's mother, greeted him warmly at the door.

"Welcome, Vasudev. Please make yourself comfortable," Geetha said with a smile. She switched on the television before heading to the kitchen. "Sakshi and I will join you shortly, once we're done in the kitchen."

Vasudev nodded and settled on the couch. He absentmindedly flipped through the TV channels but found nothing captivating. His gaze wandered around the room, landing on a series of photographs hanging on the wall. There was a serene painting of a lake, a picture of Sakshi and Geetha together, a framed image of Goddess Saraswathi, a portrait of Sakshi, and a garlanded portrait of a man. But something was missing.

"Where is Roy's picture?" Vasudev thought, puzzled. He distinctly remembered seeing a photograph of Roy on this wall during his last visit. His unease deepened.

Attempting to distract himself, he resumed surfing through the TV channels. Just then, Sakshi emerged from the kitchen, carrying a tray with a kettle and tea cups.

"Where's Roy? Shouldn't he be back from work by now?" Vasudev asked, his voice tinged with curiosity.

Sakshi paused, confused. "Roy? Who is Roy?" she asked.

"What?" Vasudev blurted out. "You don't know him? He's your husband."

Sakshi's expression grew even more puzzled. "My husband? Vasudev, I'm not married," she said, shaking her head.

Vasudev froze. His heart raced as her words echoed in his mind. *"Not married? How is that possible?"*

"Are you all right, Vasudev?" Sakshi asked, concerned. "You seem... tense."

"Oh... nothing," Vasudev stammered. "I must have been mistaken."

Before he could gather his thoughts, the evening news began on the TV. The newsreader's voice filled the room:

"Breaking news! A residence in the city was robbed at midnight yesterday, and the residents were killed in their sleep. The deceased have been identified as Mr. Roy, a travel agency proprietor, and his wife, Mrs. Anu. The suspect remains at large..."

"What?" Vasudev exclaimed, his shock barely contained. His face turned pale as he processed the announcement.

"Oh my god," Sakshi said, her eyes wide with disbelief. "That's terrible. We need to be careful. I hope the police catch the suspect soon."

Vasudev nodded nervously, his mind spiraling. "Yes... I... uh... hope so," he muttered.

Sakshi tilted her head, her concern deepening. "You were asking about someone named Roy earlier. Is he the man in the news?"

Vasudev avoided her gaze, his discomfort evident. He quickly stood up. "Sakshi, I'm sorry, but I have to go."

"What? Why?" Sakshi asked, surprised.

"I just… I think I need more rest. I should leave," Vasudev said, fumbling for an excuse.

Hearing the commotion, Geetha stepped into the hall. "Vasudev, this is your first time visiting us. I'd feel terrible if you left without spending time with us," she said kindly.

"First time?" The words struck Vasudev like a lightning bolt. *"Everything has changed."*

"Oh, uh… not a problem, aunty. I'll visit again soon," he said hastily, his voice shaky. Without waiting for further questions, he rushed out of the house and headed straight back to his own.

Vasudev slammed the door behind him, his thoughts spiraling into chaos. *"What have I done?"* He leaned heavily against the wall, trying to calm his racing heart. The reality unfolding around him felt surreal, its strangeness pressing down on him with each passing second. To ground himself, he pinched his arm—hard—confirming that this was no dream.

A wave of guilt and dread washed over him. Despite the triumph of successfully operating his time machine, the results were far from what he had envisioned. The satisfaction of achieving his scientific breakthrough was eclipsed by the unsettling changes it had wrought.

"What have I disrupted?" he thought, his mind racing. The altered events—the return of Sakshi and the death of Roy— felt like ripples of chaos caused by the stone he had thrown into the waters of time. He realized with growing horror that in his quest to rewrite his past, he might have unleashed a series of unforeseen consequences, setting off a chain of events that had now spiraled out of control.

"If I hadn't meddled with my past, none of this would be happening now," Vasudev muttered under his breath, his voice laced with regret. Yet, a spark of defiance flickered within him. "But I had no choice. I needed to use my time machine. I had to do it because of that psycho."

14. The Untold Truth

Vasudev sat before his time machine, the hum of its components filling the room. After days of effort, he had successfully repaired it, but now, a flood of uncertainty washed over him. *"What should I do next?"* he wondered, his fingers hovering over the controls.

"I must proceed cautiously this time," he thought aloud. *"The last overload nearly destroyed everything. I need to test this on something smaller, something safe."*

Determined, he decided to view events from 25 years ago. He powered up the machine, the screen flickering to life, and adjusted the electromagnetic range to precisely match his target timeframe. His fingers moved deftly as he entered a random date and time from 25 years in the past. The machine whirred as it processed the input.

"Dear God," Vasudev muttered, glancing at the faint glow of the machine's viewer. "Please let this work properly this time."

Taking a deep breath, he pressed the red button. The room grew still for a moment, and Vasudev felt his pulse quicken as he awaited the outcome of his second attempt at defying the barriers of time.

The machine roared to life, though this time with a much softer hum compared to its first chaotic run. Vasudev's heart raced as the processing percentage steadily climbed from zero. The room filled with a faint glow as the machine worked, and Vasudev leaned forward, eager to see the results of his efforts.

When the processing bar hit 100%, the sound stopped abruptly. The viewer remained blank. Vasudev's excitement gave way to frustration. He tapped the processing unit in irritation, muttering under his breath. Suddenly, the viewer flickered to life, and an image appeared.

Vasudev squinted at the scene on the screen. Two children, a boy and a girl, were arguing.

"Give this teddy bear to me! I want to play with it," the girl demanded.

"No! I want to play with this," the boy retorted.

The children tugged at the teddy bear, neither willing to let go.

"Stop fighting, both of you!" a woman's voice interrupted sharply. A lady entered the frame and stood in front of them, her hands on her hips.

Vasudev's eyes widened. *"That voice…"* he thought. As the lady spoke, his suspicions were confirmed.

"Anu, you need to be kind to your brother. Isn't he younger than you? Let him play with it for a while," the woman said sternly.

"So this is Anu's childhood," Vasudev realized. *"And that must be her younger brother, Ram. The lady… that's Neerja. My machine works perfectly!"*

The scene continued. Anu reluctantly handed the teddy bear to her brother but shoved him in anger. The boy stumbled, fell, and began crying loudly. Neerja turned her attention to the boy, scolding Anu for her behavior while consoling Ram.

Angry and frustrated, young Anu stormed out of the room.

Vasudev leaned back in his chair, a mix of satisfaction and astonishment filling his mind. His machine had succeeded in capturing a moment from the past—Anu's past. But beneath the excitement, a faint unease stirred within him. *"How much of the past do I dare to witness? And what might I uncover next?"*

Vasudev adjusted the EM range of his time machine slightly, curious to uncover more of Anu's past. The viewer flickered, revealing another scene.

Anu appeared on the screen, joyfully returning home from school with a mark sheet in her hand. "Amma, look here! I've scored 95 out of 100 in my math exam," she exclaimed, her face lit with excitement.

Neerja, standing by the door, smiled proudly. "Very good, Anu. I'm so proud of you."

Moments later, Ram entered the frame, also clutching a mark sheet. "Amma, look! I've scored a centum in my math exam," he announced with equal enthusiasm.

"Wow! Very good, Ram. That's an outstanding score," Neerja said, her pride evident.

The smile on Anu's face vanished, replaced by a flicker of jealousy. "So what," she said sharply. "I'm in the tenth grade, and he's in the sixth. His math test is simpler than mine."

Neerja's tone turned firm. "Anu, you must acknowledge your brother's achievement. He's younger than you. Why are you comparing his grades with yours?"

Anu didn't reply. Instead, she walked to her room, her expression unreadable.

Vasudev adjusted the EM range slightly.

That night, when the house was silent and everyone was asleep, Anu woke up and tiptoed into Ram's room. With a pen in hand, she vandalized his classwork notebooks, her movements deliberate. Once her task was complete, she silently crept back to her room and returned to bed, a faint smirk on her face.

Vasudev adjusted the EM range slightly again.

The next morning, Ram's distressed cries echoed through the house. Neerja rushed to his room to find him holding up his scribbled notebooks. Tears streamed down his face as he pointed to the ruined pages.

"Who did this?" Neerja asked, her voice filled with anger and concern. She immediately yelled, "Anu! Come here!"

Anu entered the room, pretending innocence. "What happened, Amma?"

Neerja showed her the notebooks, her voice rising. "Did you do this?"

Anu's expression shifted to one of anger. "I didn't do it, Amma. Why are you blaming me?"

"I know you did this, Anu. Why would you do such a thing to your own brother?" Neerja's voice trembled with a mix of anger and disappointment.

"I'm telling you I didn't do it!" Anu snapped, her tone defiant.

"You're lying!" Neerja shouted, her frustration spilling over.

Anu glared at her mother before storming back to her room, slamming the door shut. Neerja tried to console Ram, who continued sobbing over his ruined notebooks.

Meanwhile, Anu sat on her bed, her lips curling into a wicked grin. The satisfaction of her actions reflected in her eyes, a stark contrast to the pain she had left behind.

Vasudev leaned back in his chair, disturbed by what he had just witnessed. He had always known Anu to be strong-willed, but the envy and malice displayed in her childhood left him uneasy. *Was this the Anu I married?*" he wondered, his mind churning with questions.

"How can she do this to her brother? Is she mad?" Vasudev muttered to himself, disturbed by what he had just witnessed. The incident on the viewer painted Anu in a completely different light. Despite his frustration, his curiosity to uncover more about her past grew stronger. He adjusted the EM range on the machine, narrowing in on a new timeline.

The viewer flickered to life, now showing Anu seated in a college classroom. Her face was clouded with sadness, her eyes distant, lost in thought. The lecturer's words seemed to fade into the background as she remained consumed by her worries. When the class ended, Anu hurriedly packed her bag and walked home, her movements mechanical and devoid of energy.

As soon as she entered her house, she threw her bag carelessly onto the sofa and retreated to her room, shutting the door behind her with a thud. Neerja, who had been in the living room, immediately noticed her daughter's low spirits. Concerned, she followed Anu to her room and knocked softly before entering.

"What happened, Anu? Why are you so upset?" Neerja asked, her tone gentle.

Anu sat on the edge of her bed, her hands clenched into fists. "Amma, I'm worried about my semester exam results," she confessed, her voice trembling.

"Why, Anu? Didn't you do your exams well?" Neerja asked, sitting beside her.

Anu's frustration spilled out in waves. "Amma, you know I was the topper of my class during my school days. But now, I can't even secure a place in the top five! I studied day and night for my first semester exams, but when the results came out, I wasn't even in the top ten."

Neerja placed a comforting hand on her daughter's shoulder. "Anu, don't study for grades or rank," she said softly. "Study for the sake of knowledge and self-satisfaction. People might forget your rank or grades with time, but they will remember you as a knowledgeable and hardworking person."

Anu shook her head, her frustration boiling over. "I will be satisfied only if I achieve first place in my second semester results!" she declared, her tone laced with determination and fury.

Neerja sighed, sensing the intensity of Anu's ambition. "If you've worked hard and performed well, you'll definitely secure first rank, Anu. Don't stress yourself unnecessarily," she said, rising from the bed. "Now, go freshen up. You'll feel better."

As Neerja exited the room, Anu remained seated, staring blankly at the wall. Her desire for success burned fiercely, but the seeds of her insecurities seemed to grow alongside it.

Vasudev watched the scene unfold, his emotions a whirlwind. Anu's unyielding drive for perfection left him unsettled. Her struggles to reclaim her top position reflected a deeper vulnerability he hadn't noticed before.

Curious to uncover more about Anu's life, Vasudev adjusted the EM range on his time machine. The viewer flickered to life, and a new scene began to unfold. Anu was attending her class as usual the next day, her face a mix of nervousness and anticipation. The professor entered the room, his phone in hand, and announced that the second semester results had been released.

"Class, I have the rank list for your exams," the professor declared, his voice filled with excitement. He scanned the names on his phone and smiled. "Let me call someone special today."

The students watched eagerly as the professor called a boy to stand in front of the class. "Students, let's give a big round of applause for Ragul! He has not only secured the first rank in his second semester exams but has also topped the first-year exams by achieving the first rank in both consecutive semesters. This is no small feat—let's celebrate his incredible achievement!"

The classroom erupted in applause. Ragul's classmates cheered enthusiastically, some even patting him on the back. But Anu sat still, her hands frozen on her desk. She didn't clap, nor did she smile. Instead, her face twisted into a frown, disappointment and envy boiling within her.

As the professor complimented Ragul's hard work and dedication, Anu's jealousy reached its peak. She clenched her fists under the desk, her thoughts consumed by the bitterness of defeat.

Once the professor left the room, a group of students surrounded Ragul, congratulating him on his achievement. Anu couldn't bear it any longer. She reached into her bag, pulling out her steel water bottle, and walked toward Ragul.

"Congratulations," she said, forcing a smile as she shook Ragul's hand. But before anyone could react, she swung the water bottle violently, striking Ragul's head with a loud thud. Ragul collapsed to the ground, blood trickling from his head as the entire class gasped in horror. Anu fled the scene, running to hide in the girls' restroom.

Watching the incident unfold, Vasudev's heart sank. "Oh my god! Poor boy..." he muttered, shaking his head in disbelief.

The consequences of Anu's actions were swift. The college management immediately suspended her for her behavior. When Neerja and Prabhu learned of the incident, they were furious.

"What were you thinking, Anu? How could you do something so shameful?" Neerja scolded, her voice trembling with anger.

Prabhu was equally outraged. "You've embarrassed us! Do you realize how serious this is? If you don't change your ways, this will ruin your future."

They punished Anu and told her they would only approach the college to lift her suspension if she realized her mistake and promised to control her emotions. Anu, recognizing the gravity of the situation, apologized to her parents and vowed to never act out again.

A few days later, Neerja and Prabhu visited the college to plead with the management. "Please, forgive our daughter. This is her first mistake, and she deeply regrets her actions. Suspending her will disrupt her studies," Neerja pleaded.

The management, initially reluctant, eventually agreed to lift the suspension. However, they imposed strict conditions: Anu had to submit a written apology to the principal and was warned that any future misconduct would result in expulsion.

Anu returned to college a few days later, but things were not the same. Her classmates avoided her, unwilling to associate with someone whose actions had caused so much harm. She sat alone in class, isolated and shunned.

For the first time, Anu's ambition had turned against her, leaving her in a place of loneliness and regret. Watching all of this, Vasudev was left pondering the extent of Anu's insecurities and the deep scars her behavior had left on others—and herself.

"Anu never told me about this incident. I'm not sure what more she's hiding from me," Vasudev thought, his mind clouded with doubt. He couldn't shake the memory of Anu's strange behavior on the day Sakshi was killed. Determined to uncover the truth, he decided to use his time machine to see what had really happened that day.

Sitting before the machine, Vasudev adjusted the EM range to process the electromagnetic radiation from the day of Sakshi's death. He hesitated for a moment before pressing the button.

The viewer flickered to life, and an image appeared: Sakshi's house. Vasudev leaned forward, his heart pounding. The scene began to unfold.

In the kitchen, Sakshi and her mother, Geetha, were preparing food. The room was filled with the aroma of spices and the sound of utensils clinking. Suddenly, a loud knock came from the main door. Sakshi wiped her hands on her apron and rushed to open it.

When she unlocked the door, Anu stood on the threshold, her face contorted with anger.

"Oh! So, it's you. What happened, Anu?" Sakshi asked with a puzzled smile.

"Enough of you, Sakshi!" Anu snapped, her tone sharp and unrelenting.

Sakshi blinked, taken aback. "Why are you angry, Anu? First, come inside," she said, gently placing her arm on Anu's shoulder to lead her into the hall room.

But Anu pulled her arm away firmly. "I've been watching you for days now. You're trying to get close to my husband," Anu said, her voice rising with fury.

"What? What are you saying?" Sakshi asked, her confusion deepening.

"Stop acting, you… That day, you brought biriyani especially for him. Why? And to make matters worse, he even prefers your cooking over mine. I tolerated it until now, but today, you crossed the line."

"What did I do?" Sakshi asked, trying to maintain her composure.

"Why did you put your hands on my husband's shoulder?" Anu demanded, her eyes blazing.

Sakshi sighed. "Anu, you're misunderstanding everything. There's nothing going on."

"Shut up! It's you who's behaving inappropriately with Vasudev," Anu accused.

"I don't have any bad intentions, Anu. I consider Vasudev a good friend," Sakshi explained.

"Enough!" Anu yelled, shoving Sakshi with all her might.

Sakshi stumbled backward and lost her balance. Her head struck the sharp edge of the TV stand with a sickening thud.

She collapsed to the floor, motionless, as blood began pooling around her. Anu stood frozen in shock, unable to believe what she had just done.

"Oh no," Vasudev whispered, his stomach churning as he continued to watch.

Anu knelt beside Sakshi, frantically trying to wake her. But Sakshi didn't respond. Panic gripped Anu as she assumed the worst. She turned to flee the house, only to be blocked by a man standing at the main door.

He wore a black sweatshirt, black pants, and a mask that obscured his face. A knife glinted in one hand, and a gunny bag hung from his shoulder. The man froze, just as startled to see Anu as she was to see him.

Before Anu could react, the man lunged at her with the knife. She dodged, shoving him away with all her strength. Her eyes darted around the room, searching for something to defend herself. Her gaze fell on a tall wooden lamp stand near the TV.

The man clutched his head suddenly, as if struck by an excruciating headache, and stumbled. Seizing the opportunity, Anu grabbed the wooden stand and delivered a crushing blow to his head. The man dropped his knife and fell to the floor, writhing in pain. When he tried to get back up, Anu struck him again and again, until he stopped moving entirely.

"Anu…" Vasudev muttered under his breath. He couldn't believe what he was witnessing.

Breathing heavily, Anu looked at the lifeless body of the man. She remembered Geetha and began searching for her.

Geetha, who had witnessed the entire incident from the kitchen, was attempting to call the police on her phone. But before she could complete the call, Anu struck her on the head with the wooden stand. Geetha fell to the ground, unconscious.

Panting, Anu retrieved a handkerchief from her pocket and wiped her fingerprints off the wooden stand. She placed the stand in Sakshi's hand to make it appear as though Sakshi had defended herself. Without a second glance, Anu fled the house.

Vasudev sat frozen in his chair, his breath hitching as tears welled up in his eyes. The pieces of the puzzle were falling into place, but they painted a picture darker than he had imagined. The weight of the truth he had uncovered crushed him.

"Is this all true? Or is this machine faulty?" Vasudev whispered, his mind clouded with disbelief and sorrow.

Unable to bear the images anymore, he quickly turned off the machine. The room fell silent, save for the faint hum of the cooling processors. He slumped back in his chair, trying to process the horrifying events he had just witnessed.

Then, something caught his eye. A reflection on the now-blank viewer screen. He froze. It was Anu—standing right behind him, holding a knife in her hand.

Vasudev's heart raced. He shot up from his seat, facing her.

"Anu… Did you…?" Vasudev stammered, his voice trembling.

"Yes," Anu said, her voice eerily calm. "I killed both of them."

The bluntness of her confession sent a chill down Vasudev's spine. He could hardly believe his ears.

"But… why?" he managed to ask, still reeling.

"I didn't want to kill them," Anu said, her voice trembling for the first time. "It was an accident."

"No," Vasudev said, shaking his head. His tone shifted, anger lacing his words. "It was not an accident. I saw everything. You were trying to cover up your crime as well."

"It wasn't like that!" Anu shouted, her eyes flashing with anger. "I just wanted to negotiate with her. Things… spiraled out of control. It wasn't my fault!" Her voice broke, but then she smirked coldly. "So, what's next? You're going to call the cops, aren't you?"

"No, Anu," Vasudev said firmly, his voice steady despite the chaos in his mind. "You don't need the police. You need a doctor. It's clear—you're mentally ill."

The words struck like a hammer. Anu's smirk vanished, replaced by an expression of pure rage.

"You think I'm mentally ill, don't you?" she hissed. "I did everything for you because I love you!"

Vasudev stepped back, his hands raised defensively. "You are… mentally… unstable… for sure."

Anu's lips curled into a deranged smile. "Hmm… Yes… Yes… I am!" she screamed, her voice echoing in the room.

Before Vasudev could react, Anu lunged at him with the knife.

Anu's sudden lunge caught Vasudev off guard. The blade gleamed as it hurtled toward him. Instinct took over, and Vasudev jumped aside just in time. The knife missed him by inches, embedding itself into the chair he had been sitting on moments before.

"Anu! Stop this madness!" Vasudev yelled, backing away, his hands trembling.

But Anu was relentless. She yanked the knife out of the chair and turned to him, her eyes wild with fury. "You called me mentally ill! After everything I've done for you! For us!" she screamed, advancing toward him.

Vasudev stumbled backward, his mind racing for a way to diffuse the situation. "Anu, please, listen to me," he pleaded, his voice shaking. "This isn't you. You're not thinking clearly."

"I'm thinking more clearly than ever," Anu snarled, gripping the knife tightly. "You're the one who's blind. You can't see how much I've sacrificed for you. For us to be together."

Her words stung, but Vasudev couldn't let them cloud his judgment. He glanced around the room, searching for something—anything—that could help him defend himself. His eyes fell on the lamp on the table nearby.

"I don't want to hurt you, Anu," Vasudev said, slowly edging toward the lamp. "But you need to stop this."

Anu let out a bitter laugh. "Hurt me? You can't hurt me, Vasudev. You don't have it in you."

In a swift motion, Anu lunged again, aiming for his chest. Vasudev grabbed the lamp and swung it with all his might. The lamp struck Anu's hand, knocking the knife to the ground. She screamed in pain and clutched her wrist.

"Stop it, Anu. You're too dangerous to be left free. I have no choice but to call the cops now," Vasudev said, his voice rising in anger.

"No, please don't call the cops!" Anu begged, her eyes wide with desperation.

"I will!" Vasudev said firmly, pushing her toward a corner.

Anu stood motionless for a moment, her head lowered. Slowly, she lifted her face and locked eyes with Vasudev. A chilling silence filled the room before she suddenly burst into laughter.

Vasudev froze, startled by her reaction.

"I know. You won't listen to me because you never truly loved me," Anu said, her laughter fading into a bitter smile. "I wanted us to enjoy a beautiful life together here in Andaman... but you...you never cared about me."

Before Vasudev could respond, Anu pulled out her phone. "What are you doing?" he asked, his voice tinged with alarm.

Anu dialled 100 and waited as the call connected.

"Hello," Inspector Varun's voice came through.

"Hello, this is Anu, Vasudev's wife," she said, her tone calm but filled with venom. "I want to report that my husband, Vasudev, is the one who killed Sakshi and that man at Roy's house. He lied to you."

"What?" Vasudev shouted in disbelief, stepping forward to snatch the phone, but Anu turned away, continuing her accusations.

"That day, he wasn't in Marina Park. He was at Sakshi's house. I was the sole witness. He tied my hands and mouth and locked me in the bathroom to keep me silent."

"Stop it, Anu!" Vasudev yelled, grabbing at the phone, but she ended the call before he could take it from her.

Breathing heavily, Vasudev glared at her. "Why would you do this? I'll call Varun and tell him the truth right now!" he shouted, reaching for his phone.

Before he could dial, Anu picked up the knife from the floor and, with a wild look in her eyes, plunged it into her abdomen.

Vasudev froze, his face pale with horror. "Anu! What are you doing?" he screamed.

Ignoring his cries, Anu pulled the knife out and stabbed herself again. Blood spilled onto the floor as Vasudev rushed toward her, trying to wrest the knife from her hand. But it was too late.

Anu collapsed to the ground, her body shaking as she bled profusely. Vasudev's hands were stained red as he knelt beside her, the bloodied knife finally in his grasp.

Time seemed to stand still as he stared at Anu's pale, trembling form.

"I won't go to jail. You will go. The cops will be here any moment now," Anu whispered with her final breath, her voice fading into a chilling calmness. "I've been watching you since the day we came to Andaman. You love Sakshi, don't you? You even prefer her biryani over mine. You will... now... suffer."

Her words struck Vasudev like a thunderbolt. He dropped the knife in horror and stared at his bloodied hands, trembling. Anu's lifeless body lay before him, and the echo of her accusations filled the room.

Panic surged through him. "What do I do now?" he thought, pacing the blood-stained floor. He knew Varun would be there any minute, and Anu's call had already sealed his fate.

Vasudev stopped, his eyes darting to the time machine. A sudden realization dawned upon him. "I can use this machine," he muttered to himself. "I can replay what just happened and prove my innocence."

But there was a problem. "The machine doesn't have a recording feature," Vasudev realized, running his hands through his hair. "How will I capture the incident?"

He glanced at his phone and an idea struck him. "I can use the phone's camera to record the events displayed on the viewer," he thought, grabbing his phone. "But calibrating the machine to extract such a recent event... that's the real challenge."

He switched on the machine, adjusting the EM range with one hand while holding his phone camera in the other. His fingers worked frantically, his heart pounding in his chest.

"The EM rays from a recent event are too mixed up with rays from several other recent events," Vasudev muttered. "Extracting one specific event is like finding a needle in a haystack."

He paused to steady himself, recalling a concept he had read about. "Think of white light. It contains seven colors, but they're indistinguishable to the naked eye. When the light is dispersed, the colors separate and become visible. Similarly, recent EM rays are like undispersed white light—intertwined and chaotic. But older events... their rays are dispersed across the universe, making them easier to extract."

He exhaled, narrowing his focus. "I need precision. Just a few minutes ago… it's possible." His hands adjusted the dials meticulously, fine-tuning the EM range to isolate the critical moment.

The viewer began to flicker, faint images appearing and disappearing in bursts of static. Vasudev clenched his jaw, sweat dripping down his forehead. "Come on… just a little more…" he whispered.

The room was heavy with tension as the machine whirred, the faint glow of the viewer casting shadows on the walls. He knew this was his only chance to prove his innocence.

Vasudev's hands trembled as he continued tuning the EM range. The viewer flickered, and an image began to form. On the screen, he saw himself clutching a bloodied knife, staring at Anu, who was collapsing to the ground, bleeding profusely from her abdomen. And then, abruptly, the screen went black.

His heart sank. "What is this?" he muttered. "Where's the part where Anu confesses and stabs herself?"

He picked up his phone, where he had just recorded the displayed footage. After watching the brief clip, Vasudev, stunned and confused, deleted it. "This doesn't prove my innocence—it only makes me look guiltier."

Desperate, he re-tuned the EM range, attempting to recover the scene where Anu admitted her crimes and stabbed herself. But no matter how much he adjusted the machine, the incident didn't reappear. Frustrated, Vasudev switched to the date of Sakshi's death, intending to record the moment Anu murdered Sakshi and the thief. Again, he failed.

A horrifying realization dawned upon him. "Once the rays of an event are processed and visualized, they can't be retrieved again," Vasudev muttered, slumping into his chair. His head spun with the weight of the truth: he had no evidence to prove his innocence.

He was cornered. "What can I do now?" he whispered, staring at his hands. His gaze shifted around the room, and it landed on Anu's lifeless body.

"The root of all my problems…" he thought. His heart raced as an idea began to form. "If I eliminate the root, I eliminate the problem."

The wearable device on his wrist caught his attention. Vasudev had designed it to transport a person through time, but he had never dared to use it due to the risks. But now, desperation left him no choice. He contemplated traveling back to Anu's past—to stop her from ever entering his life.

A plan began to take shape in his mind. Before he could finalize his decision, a sudden knock at the main door shattered his thoughts. His blood ran cold.

Someone was outside.

15. Dealing with the Present

Vasudev sat on the couch, staring at the machine he had built with years of relentless effort. His mind was clouded with the weight of the lives affected by his actions. He sighed deeply and whispered, "I apologize, Mr. Roy. None of this was supposed to happen. May your soul find peace." Slowly, he rose and walked toward the machine, his heart heavy with conflicting emotions.

"Today, my years of hard work will finally pay off," Vasudev thought, placing his hands on the controls. His fingers hesitated before turning the knobs. He entered the necessary inputs and began tuning the EM range.

Suddenly, he froze. A wave of doubt washed over him. "Is this the right thing to do? If I make this change, will it solve my problem? Or will it spiral into something far worse?"

He paused to reflect. "Our present is shaped by the actions of our past. Every decision we make creates ripples, determining the course of our future. This phenomenon is what we call the butterfly effect. Even a small change in the past can create an unimaginable impact on the future—sometimes for the better, but often for the worse. And once the change is made, there's no turning back."

Vasudev clenched his fists. "When I altered my past to stop my marriage, I unintentionally set off a chain reaction. Anu married Roy. That led her to Andaman, where she was killed during the robbery. And Roy, an innocent man, lost his life too. Indirectly, their deaths are on me."

The weight of his guilt made him pause. "What if I go back further? What if I stop my father from borrowing money for his business? Would that solve everything? Maybe he would've continued running the grocery store, and Swathi might still be alive… But what if something worse happened instead? My family endured pain, but it made us stronger. Perhaps that was our fate."

He took a deep breath, his eyes welling up with tears. "Fate." The word echoed in his mind. "Everything happens as part of a larger plan—God's plan. My family's struggles, my sister's death—they were all meant to be. The past is unchangeable, no matter how much I wish otherwise. What truly matters is the present."

Vasudev looked at his machine, his masterpiece, with a mixture of pride and dread. "This machine is dangerous. It has already caused so much damage. In the wrong hands, it could bring about untold chaos. I can't allow that to happen."

He stepped back, his resolve firm. "I've had enough of time travel. This machine is a curse disguised as a blessing. It must be destroyed."

With trembling hands, Vasudev picked up an iron rod from the storeroom. Standing before his creation, his heart pounded with a mix of relief and sorrow. *"This ends now,"* he thought. He raised the rod and swung it down with all his might, smashing the processing unit into shards. The receiver dish bent and cracked under the force of his blows. The viewer screen shattered into countless fragments, scattering across the floor like broken dreams.

Vasudev continued to thrash the machine, his arms moving furiously as sweat dripped from his brow. The metallic echoes of destruction reverberated through the house. He didn't stop until the machine was reduced to a pile of unrecognizable rubble, beyond any chance of repair.

Panting and drenched, Vasudev slumped into his chair. He looked at the shattered remains of his time machine with a strange sense of relief. For the first time in a long while, he felt lighter, as if the burden of time itself had been lifted off his shoulders. A faint smile appeared on his face.

Moments later, his cellphone rang, breaking the silence. Vasudev took it out of his pocket and answered, "Hello?"

"Hello, Vasu. How are you? You haven't spoken to me in such a long time," came Nirmala's warm, familiar voice.

"Ma…" Vasudev replied, his voice tinged with joy. "I'm fine, Ma. How are you?"

"I'm good, Vasu. But I was a little worried. You've been so busy with your project that you didn't even call us. How's it going? Weren't you supposed to present it at the national science conference in Port Blair?" Nirmala asked.

Vasudev froze for a moment, his mind racing. *"What conference?...Oh, wait,"* he thought, as the realization hit him. The timeline had been altered due to his time travel, changing the very purpose of his visit to the islands. He was no longer married to Anu, and the conference was likely part of a different version of events. Quickly composing himself, he adjusted his response to his mother.

"Well...actually...my project is a failure," Vasudev admitted.

"Why, Vasu? What happened?" Nirmala asked, her concern evident.

"It didn't work as I expected, Ma. So, I decided to drop the idea of presenting it at the conference," Vasudev said.

There was a pause before Nirmala spoke, her voice filled with encouragement. "Don't worry, Vasu. Failure is just a stepping stone. Keep trying, and don't give up too soon."

"Thanks, Ma. But it's okay. I'll figure things out. You don't need to worry," Vasudev said, a genuine warmth in his tone.

"Wait a minute," Nirmala said. "Your father wants to talk to you."

After a few seconds, Selvam's cheerful voice came through the line. "Hello, Vasu! I hope you didn't forget about me."

"Stop kidding, Appa," Vasudev replied, chuckling.

"I heard your conversation with Nirmala. So your project didn't work, huh? What's next?" Selvam asked with concern.

Vasudev hesitated for a moment before replying, "Actually, I'm planning a vacation."

"What?" Selvam asked, surprised.

"You heard me right, Appa. I'm planning to explore the Andaman and Nicobar Islands. I think it's time for a little sightseeing," Vasudev said, a newfound determination in his voice.

Selvam chuckled. "That's a good idea, Vasu. You deserve a break."

As the call ended, Vasudev leaned back in his chair, staring at the ruins of his creation. He had decided to leave the past behind and focus on living in the moment.

16. Aftermath

Vasudev returned to his hometown a week later, settling back into the comforting rhythm of life with his parents. He resumed his role as a professor, sharing his passion for theoretical physics with his students. A week after his return, he celebrated his mother's birthday with grandeur, cherishing the joy of being reunited with his family.

Despite his efforts to move on, the shadows of his past lingered in his mind. Nightmares of his time in Andaman and the unintended consequences of his actions haunted him. To find peace, Vasudev turned to meditation and yoga, striving to let go of his regrets and embrace the present.

He never remarried. Reflecting on his tumultuous experiences, he chose to dedicate his life to caring for his parents and finding happiness in their company. Though content, a pang of guilt remained for his indirect role in Mr. Roy's death—a burden he quietly carried.

Vasudev maintained a warm bond with Sakshi's family, grateful for their hospitality during his stay in Andaman. Even after returning home, he stayed in touch, often calling Sakshi and her mother to check on their well-being.

One day, Vasudev ventured into a nearby forest with a bag in hand. He wandered deep into the woods until he found a secluded spot. Setting the bag down, he unzipped it and emptied its contents onto the ground. Out tumbled books, papers filled with formulas, and detailed instructions for building the time machine. Alongside them was a bottle of kerosene and a matchbox.

Without hesitation, Vasudev doused the papers and books with kerosene, striking a match to ignite the pile. He stood silently, watching the flames consume the remnants of his dangerous invention. As the fire crackled and the papers turned to ash, a light smile formed on his face.

After a while, Vasudev turned and walked back home, feeling a sense of closure and relief as he left the burning past behind.

Sakshi's rental house welcomed new neighbors, a friendly family who quickly discovered her culinary talent—particularly her famous biryani. It didn't take long for the aroma of Sakshi's cooking to make its way to their home, sparking curiosity and appetite. True to her generous nature, Sakshi made sure to share her biryani with her new neighbors every time she prepared it.

The simple act of sharing food soon blossomed into regular conversations over tea and laughter-filled evenings. With each passing day, their bond grew stronger, evolving from friendly exchanges to a meaningful connection. Over time, Sakshi and her neighbors became inseparable, building a relationship rooted in kindness, trust, and, of course, delicious biryani.

A few weeks later...

The Coast Guard intercepted a man attempting to flee the Andaman Islands in a fishing boat under the cover of night. The suspect was apprehended and handed over to the local police for questioning. Though he was unable to speak, he managed to communicate by jotting down his statements.

Further investigation revealed that the suspect had a criminal history and was already implicated in a robbery case in Chennai. Evidence tied him to the murder of two individuals during that robbery. The suspect was tried, convicted, and sentenced to life imprisonment in the Central Prison in Chennai.

As he languished behind bars, he spent his days reflecting on his shattered dreams and missed opportunities. Yet, amidst the gloom of his cell, he found a twisted sense of satisfaction—he had exacted vengeance on the person he blamed for his ruined life, the person who, in his eyes, was responsible for his inability to speak and the collapse of his ambitions. It was a grim consolation for a life spent in regret and bitterness.

Our lives are shaped by the way we choose to live, regardless of wealth or status. What truly matters are our deeds, for they ultimately define the essence of our existence. However, doing

good deeds does not ensure a life free from challenges. Problems and hardships are an integral part of the human journey. While we cannot escape them, we can find the courage and resilience to confront them.

Often, the trials we face or the events unfolding around us are a result of our own actions. Every decision we make, no matter how small, has a ripple effect on our lives. Everything happens for a reason, even if the reason isn't immediately clear. Life grants us the freedom to choose our paths, but it also holds us accountable for the consequences of those choices. Understanding this balance is key to navigating the complexities of existence.

A few months later,

In Central Prison, Chennai.

The dimly lit corridors echoed with the sound of heavy boots as a prison officer made his nightly inspection rounds. Tasked with overseeing the custody and discipline of inmates, he stopped abruptly in front of a cell. Inside, Ragul lay on the floor, his legs crossed and arms tucked behind his head, staring blankly at the cracked ceiling.

The officer frowned, tapping his baton against the cold iron bars with a loud clang. "Hey! What's this pose? Sit up properly!" he barked, his voice sharp and commanding.

Ragul didn't move. He remained motionless, his eyes fixed on the ceiling as though he hadn't heard a thing.

The officer grew irritated. "I'm talking to you, mute boy! What are you daydreaming about, huh?" he shouted.

Still, there was no response. Ragul's silence was unsettling, almost defiant.

The officer smirked cruelly. "Oh, I get it. You're mute, so you can't answer me. Well, let me tell you something. Whatever you're thinking about doesn't matter. Your life is over. You'll rot in this cell till the end of your days. Your suffering has only just begun!"

With a menacing laugh, he struck the baton against the bars one last time before walking away, his footsteps fading into the dark corridor.

Ragul's red eyes burned with anger. Slowly, he turned his head towards the cell gate. He glared at the retreating figure of the officer, his gaze piercing and unyielding. The officer's words had pierced through him like a knife. After a few moments, he turned back to the ceiling, his face a mask of suppressed rage and despair. He slowly closed his eyes, trying to bury his thoughts.

Suddenly, the ground beneath him began to tremble. The faint rattle of the cell gate turned into a loud, clanging sound. Ragul opened his eyes in shock and sat up quickly. The entire prison started to shake violently. An earthquake.

Sirens blared across the facility as prisoners shouted in fear and confusion. Guards ran down the corridors, shouting orders.

"Everyone stay inside your cells! Do not panic!" a senior officer yelled over the commotion.

Lights flickered erratically, casting eerie shadows on the prison walls. Dust and debris fell from the ceiling, and the sound of cracking concrete echoed through the halls. Ragul gripped the bars of his cell, staring out at the chaos. His usual calm was replaced by an expression of unease.

The prison authorities scrambled to assess the situation, initiating emergency protocols to ensure the safety of both inmates and staff. Guards moved quickly, unlocking cells in areas at risk of structural collapse and relocating prisoners to safer parts of the facility. Ragul was among those ordered to evacuate his cell.

As he stepped out into the corridor, his expression changed—no longer anger, but a strange calmness, as if the earthquake had shaken loose something deeper within him. The tremors eventually subsided, leaving an eerie silence in their wake, broken only by the distant sound of alarms and panicked voices.

Ragul glanced around, his eyes narrowing as he observed the chaos. His lips curled ever so slightly, forming a faint, enigmatic smile before he followed the guards to safety.

About the Author

S Ashvin

S. Ashvin, a mechanical engineer by profession, is the author of the science-fiction novel "Once Upon a Time in Andaman." His passion for reading and writing sci-fi stories began during his school days. Inspired by numerous sci-fi tales, writing a novel was always a dream of his, which he fulfilled with the publication of "Once Upon a Time in Andaman." He is currently working on his next novel. When not immersed in crafting his next story or enjoying the latest sci-fi thriller, Ashvin loves dancing, long-distance running, spending time with friends and family, and playing video games. He resides in Coimbatore with his family.

You can connect with the author on:

Instagram: instagram.com/cpl_ashvin

Twitter: twitter.com/officialashvin1

E-mail: ashvin.karthick.99@gmail.com

www.ingramcontent.com/pod-product-compliance
Lightning Source LLC
Chambersburg PA
CBHW021203130726
47988CB00002B/495